I0670436

A Fire to Kindle

BOOK 1 OF THE SPIRIT WIND SERIES

DANIEL DYDEK

BEORN

BEORN PUBLISHING, LLC

Copyright © 2023 by Daniel Dydek

Cover Design by GetCovers, www.getcovers.com

Published by Beorn Publishing, LLC

Canton, OH

www.beornpublishing.com

All Scripture quotes come from the King James Bible, part of the public domain.

Formatting by Atticus

All rights reserved. This book or any portion thereof may not be reproduced or used in any manner whatsoever without the express written permission of the author except for the use of brief quotations in a book review or scholarly journal.

This is a work of fiction. Names, characters, places, events, and incidents are either the products of the author's imagination or used in a fictitious manner. Any resemblance to actual persons, living or dead, or actual events is purely coincidental.

ISBN-13: 979-8-9874621-5-7

Dedication

For Playlist Makers, and God,
who can inspire an entire story
in an hour

Dedication

Contents

Chapter 1

Normally, I loved tending to the catacombs beneath our convent. Often dark, but rarely dank, the walls and alcoves brimmed with history and religion. Sister Lucy told me often the stories of the most important dead—well, they were important to me. She made a frequent and hard point that all were equal before The Beloved. But some had done deeds so much more brave and selfless and heroic that I could not help but admire them more. Whenever it was my turn to bring the incense and pray, I'm sorry if I sought out particular ones, and perhaps prayed there more fervently.

But today had not been normal, so far. The candle I brought with me guttered constantly. I worried it was one I had cast, had been lazy or inattentive when I made the wax and all sorts of impurities had gotten in—or, more properly, hadn't been gotten out. It looked perfectly fine, to me. And yet it weakly fought off the shadows from corners and holes, and I tripped constantly on the uneven floor.

I think that's how I got lost. Between the tripping and the shadows and the worrying about what my hem might look like by the time I returned, I looked up once and didn't recognize the passage where I stood. I traced over the walls with my eyes, seeing names I had never read before. Part of my job was to clean out the dust and cobwebs, too; but the task had not been done in months, it looked to me. Except behind me, where I now could see clearly the trail of my dress. I would be scolded for that, for certain.

I should have gone straight back the way I came. On a normal day, I would have. But something kept me. I thought it was merely curiosity—a trait not completely gotten out of me by the Sisters. Well, they had tried their best, but it had only been a few months so far. As I stood there in the warring shadows, my eyes kept drifting further into the dark, into the undisturbed dust. Why had no one gone that way in so long?

I took a step further in, and in my mind I thought I felt—a presence? A hum? Then, and now, I cannot tell, though I have suspicions. I might have had one last chance to decide to turn back, but I didn't. What I know for certain is that, by the second step, I was trapped. I know that now.

In the moment, I only knew my little candle struggled more at times, and at others blazed forward brighter than a torch. The catacombs here were clearly even older. The letters carved in the faces were better-worn and more angular, the dust in them lay thicker. It smelled earthier, less like stone and wax and more like mushrooms and leaf mold. In my head I saw fleeting and dancing visions of whirling druid circles. There was a strange thrill in me, like when I would stand at the edge of the bell-tower and look down to the flagstones far below.

The visions came more frequently with each breath, each time the scents swirled through my nose—now of holly and elm. The longer they lingered, the more I saw in them—there was some festival going on in the moonlight. Drums thumped like heartbeats. Men and women ululated or sang in otherworldly, guttural tongues. I had heard that tongue once before, when pale men in thick beards and braids had stopped by our convent for an evening. I wasn't supposed to, but I heard them talking in low voices after supper in their own language. It frightened me, then. It sounded like a language forged from violence. But in song...

So I must be forgiven, as these visions glowed and pulsed, that I thought the music was simply part of this dream festival. It took time until I realized the music was there even when the visions were gone for a moment. Only when it grew louder than the visions.

I stopped walking. The scents and visions faded for a moment, and there was only the music. One instrument, a harp. But softer and not as...plucky. Like they weren't being created by a harp string. More like each note already existed and could simply be heard when it was supposed to be. And it seemed far distant, as if the song came to me from across far hills, now stronger, now quieter, as the wind carried it to me.

It was only then I began to actually feel the entrapment I think I entered into with that second step. Because suddenly I wanted to go, to leave the music far behind and find the Sisters and ask what this place was and what was happening to me. But I couldn't. The desperation grew in me as the visions and music had: slowly at first, increasing desperately as I felt more and more the invisible shackles. It peaked when I tried to turn my head back the way I had come, and could not.

The wind upon which the music came grew more violent. It was my own breathing as I gasped my panic. The drums thumped faster. The dancers whirled swifter than any human limbs could possibly move. Their eyes grew wide in desperation as they felt the entrapment of my imagination. Their limbs were shackled, too, the strings leading to my mind, their movements entwined to my panic. Soon, no matter how I moved them, their desperate eyes found mine and they begged silently for me to release them, but I could not.

I could not let them go, as I could not be let go. But I could let the panic go. I focused on this. I forced myself to breathe deeply. I stopped trying to turn back. I stopped trying to move altogether, and let myself live in the moment I had found myself. Slowly I consoled myself that I was here whether I willed it now or not, and the only way out was acceptance or death. I didn't like it, knew it was not something I should harbor. It was that attitude that had brought me to the Sisters in the first place.

The panic rose again, briefly, but I fought it down again. The drums slowed. The dancers moved slower and with grace. Their eyes thanked me, and the joy of the dance returned. The harp-wind came gently, the soft strains and notes soothed the way they had at first.

Movement came back to me. I looked down at the dust, previously undisturbed ahead of me. There were tracks, now, made with tiny little feet with long toes and claws. On the left side of the passage, the toes all pointed toward me, and were sharp and clear and I could almost count the number of those who made them. But on the right side the tracks were indistinct as though the rats had departed swiftly.

I still cannot recall seeing them. But I knew they had come and gone while I stood there. Some hoard of rats, perhaps dozens, had come while I was entrapped, watched me as I fought my panic, then left swiftly in a mad rush as I came out of it, almost as though they feared what I might do to them when I became...

Free. I could move fully again, even look behind me. I think at this point I could have chosen anything I wished. So it was again the curiosity not quite gotten out of me that extended my hand with the candle to try to read some of the names of the interred. I would have to ask the Sisters about this place, and hope they would know of it by the names. The crypts were older than them—I knew some parts of it were—but I knew they had learned about much of it, in various ways.

I now wish I had not been so curious. But it is too late for that. Here is what I read:

Bartimaeus of Holden. Worship of demons, letting of blood, strangling of two children, known. Buried without his head and hands.

Percival of Holden. Worship of demons and stars, sacrifice of white bulls, stoning of three monks, known. Buried without his head and hands.

Garrett of Holden. Worship of trees, letting of blood for sacrifice, hanging entrails of three monks, known. Buried without his head and hands.

Bruce of Holden. Worship of demons and demigods; offering of dismembered women and children; performing Blood Eagle on women, children, and clergy; abuse of women, children, and corpses for carnal pleasure. Buried without head, hands, feet, or left ribs. Consigned by monks to eternal purgatory at the edge of the Lake of Fire, in torment of flames and with unending and unrealized hope of salvation.

I realized I was praying. My eyes read the inscriptions over and over, and my feet shuffled closer. My head bowed as though being pulled by invisible threads toward the tomb of Bruce of Holden. To my horror, I realized I was praying for his salvation.

As soon as I recognized the words coming from my mouth in holiest Latin, the threads broke and I ran. Fleetingly, from the corner of my eye as I turned, I swear I saw a single pair of gleaming eyes like a rat, watching me with solemnity.

I did not stop until I reached again the stairs leading up to the surface. My candle had gone out. I don't know how I saw where I was going. Here, though, enough steady and pleasant light peered down from the still-open door for me to see.

I wrung my hands. Something was on them, clinging. I thought it to be cobwebs. In the light, they were clean, but I know I felt something that wouldn't come off. Perhaps with a harsh lye. I would have to be careful of my sleeves—

The cuffs were red with blood. I looked further down; my hem that I was worried would be dusty was drenched red as well. And yet my slippers were clean. I think it was that detail alone that saved me from the panic rising again, because it was so strange my mind wouldn't let go of it. I froze at the top of the stairs, on the threshold of the sacristy. I once appreciated the cleansing feeling it gave my spirit to walk among the sacred objects after walking so long among the dead; now I feared I would sully it all. I minced through, hurrying only as I neared the opposite door and nearly bolted into the cloister.

I needed to talk to Sister Lucy first. Well, before any others. Before that I would need to change my dress. If she believed me, calmed my fears or at least explained them, I might show her the dress. Of course, it wouldn't be as simple as that, because I didn't have another dress. That was a luxury reserved for full Sisters, not acolytes in their first year before taking vows.

As it turned out, I needn't have worried. I had been so long in the catacombs that I had missed Scuros prayers, and found Sister Lucy waiting for me in my cell. (I still hate that name, because it sounds like a prison. Perhaps it would seem so by the end of the year, before I could enter the Sisters' Dormitories, but at the time it wasn't like that for me.)

I stood there far more calmly than I felt, waiting for her brows to climb back down from their perch, or for her to speak, or run out screaming, or something. She took a breath.

"Child, where have you been?"

The simplicity of the question startled me, and I looked at her like a pouting child afraid to admit a mistake.

"You should have been back from the catacombs an hour ago," she prodded.

Had it been that long? Clearly. What could I tell her? How much might she understand, or how much might she take for the flights of an unsettled mind? It occurred to me to find out how much she might already know. I cleared my throat.

"I am sorry, Sister," I began quietly—I admit, timidly. I think I had the right. "I became lost, and wandered somehow into a passage I had never seen before. It seemed like no one had been there—" My eyes came up, and I saw a strange expression on her face. Almost as if she knew already what I was talking about. I shut my mouth and waited for her to speak.

"The catacombs are a strange place," she said softly. Her eyes darted to the garden and back. "There are certainly alcoves to which I have never been, and no mortal soul should go." Her voice held a question, and I was impelled to answer.

"There were several men, all from Holden—" I broke off again, this time from a sharp *tsk!* from Sister Lucy, and a swift cut with her hand.

She drew a deep sigh. "Rae-Anna, that was a most terrible place to find yourself lost."

You're telling me...

"How did you find yourself there?"

Hesitantly, with as few details as I could get by, I told her. Her eyes constantly flicked to the garden and back, as though watching for someone. In some corner of my mind, I imagined she watched for Sister Judith. Not that either of us should be afraid of her, but after only a few months I knew her to be very severe.

When I finished the story, I expected—hoped—for some explanation from her. She looked me up and down and clasped her hands again. "Well," she said in normal tones, as though I had only told her how I had spent an afternoon in the countryside. "We must get the soil from your dress before supper. Off with us, to the washroom."

I blinked, but she gave me no chance to ask questions as she swept from the cell, striding along the cloister—the long sheltered walk that surrounded the square garden—toward the washroom on the north wall. I glanced again at my cuffs and hem, saw the blood splashed there, and shuddered. She was not wrong—except she called it soil?

"Sister," I asked, trembling anew as I caught up to her. "Where would blood have come from?"

Her steps faltered as she looked at me, clearly and honestly startled. "Blood?" she asked, her voice rising before she caught it and lowered it again. She gave a short, nervous chuckle as we continued on. "Clay can become very red, child, but it does not make it blood."

We arrived at the washroom, and I stared at my dress. Despite her assurance, it looked very much like blood to me. I had seen clay stains before, those naturally gotten from playing where my mother used to scold me. And though, true, sometimes quite red, it was not the scarlet of what was on my pale sleeves now. And not with the appearance of splashing that I saw.

"Come, off with it," Sister Lucy said sternly as I gaped like a fish.

I complied, and began scrubbing it in our washbasin. I trembled now from the cold; Sister Lucy made no comment, probably believing it proper penance for me to stand in a shift. The stains, as they came out, turned the most ordinary brown in the water, and I clenched my teeth.

"This will take too long to dry, in this weather," Sister Lucy said. "Back to your cell, and stay in your blankets until supper. I will explain your absence to the others."

Though they sounded to my ear as words of departing, she followed me back along the cloister and watched as I wrapped myself in the coarse wool blankets. She stood framed in the doorway of evening light, a faint nimbus around her head like the Mother, and I felt calm again. And I began to think.

"Sister," I began, as she still made no move to leave. "Why are there men buried under there? And why those men? Why were they not..." I wasn't entirely sure how such evil men should have been disposed of.

"Burned?"

I shrugged.

"For your first question, let me ask you: why is there an empty forge across the way?"

Forge? Oh. "Where we keep our bolts of cloth?" I asked.

Sister Lucy only raised an eyebrow.

"I guess I noticed the fireplace..."

"And an anvil?" she remarked drily.

I smiled sheepishly. "Well, that too. I guess I never wondered why."

"You were never told?"

I shook my head.

"I am getting more forgetful each year," she said with a sigh. "I hope I shall never forget The Beloved." She appeared startled by her own statement, but recollected herself. "This was once a monastery, not a convent. It makes do for our needs, well enough. But that is why there are remains of men."

I felt my heart race. "They were monks?"

Sister Lucy became somber. "There are none who are free from the enticements of the world," she said. "Even the most devout struggle daily in the battle with demons. The greater the soul, the greater the temptations that must meet them. Envy not, dear child, the faith of those before you; for such temptations as they faced would overwhelm you in an instant."

"But...to do so to women and children...after all else they must have done... And so why not destroy them completely? Why save them, so others might see their deeds..." Even as I said it, I began to understand.

Sister Lucy must have noticed, for she only nodded as though we both agreed. "Well spoken, child: so we all might see their deeds, and beware."

"But the place had not seen the step of a foot for..." I trailed off again. I hadn't told her about the rats.

At this, she sighed heavily. "There are always reasons, are there not. In truth, strange things happened down there, long ago. Long before my time, and the time of her before me. It was passed down to me that a Sister had lost her mind, visiting there. She saw visions," she continued, looking hard at me; I had told her about those, though not in detail. "And she heard—"

"Music," I said, feeling faint. I had left that out, too, and now wished...I don't know what I wished. Of all the Sisters, I trusted Lucy the most, and wanted her to know. I wished that it had not happened. Silly.

"What did you hear?" she asked. Her voice held no note of fear or condemnation. It was why I trusted her. She only wanted me to tell.

"It seemed like a harp," I said. "Except, when someone plays a harp, you can hear them pluck the strings. This seemed like the notes just...like I simply became aware of them at the proper time."

Her brows furrowed as she considered me. Slowly her eyes went distant, then came back. "There is an instrument I have heard of from far to the north, across the sea, and again even farther north upon land: an aeolian harp. Where the winds blow the strongest, they blow hard enough to tremble the strings. As the winds alter in speed, they will play upon different strings. I have never heard it, but descriptions sound similar."

She hesitated as if hearing the music, and fearing. "But, child, of greater concern to me is that I have heard no stories of that harp except one: that a single of these instruments had made its way down the southern roads, across the sea, in some strange merchant's baggage, and through the shadowed woods. It was said, in the story, that it was in those woods it received its evil enchantments. But this was said only after it had been purchased and played by—and had driven mad—a man from the nearby village."

"But how did he play it, if it is played by the winds?" A fear had begun to gnaw on me that I didn't wish to be spoken aloud. I asked this only to delay it as long as possible.

"He had made a bow, much like you would play a violin, but it produced a far different sound. In the story, he claimed he had used flax or camelhair or ox hair—it changes with the telling. But, the story concludes, it was in truth made from the new hair of infants, that nothing else could play the strings as softly."

We waited in silence. As if sensing what was unspoken, the winds outside picked up and a scattering of leaves swirled across the garden, clattering like old bones.

"Who was it?" I asked—again knowing we both knew the answer. But the wind called for it to be spoken aloud.

"Bruce," she said. "Of Holden."

Just then our gate bell rang, and I couldn't contain a short shriek. Sister Lucy seemed momentarily startled as well, but then grinned. "Someone seeks entrance," she said gently. "Of true flesh and blood, I've no doubt. Put on your dress, child, and answer our door?"

Chapter 2

I quickly obeyed, though the dress was still damp in a few uncomfortable spots. My own body would dry it soon, and so I smoothed my hair and tried to banish all thoughts of Bruce of Holden (I failed) as I made my way through the garden. It was difficult to call it a garden this time of year. The trees, bereft of foliage, were stark and thin-limbed; the few bushes and shrubs sat still in even the harshest wind. Everything else was rocks, flagstones, and a few benches, all cold and uninviting as a winter's day though it was only autumn. I passed quickly through to the gate and opened the grate.

Of anyone who might come to visit or call, the one I saw was not who I wished. Well, maybe a part of me did, but not just now. A bag over one shoulder, simple brown trews and gray shirt on his lean but sturdy body, his brown hair gathered back in a small tail, his flashing hazel eyes...

Sister Judith would have been appalled with me. "Oh, hello Thomas," I faltered. "I wasn't expecting—we weren't expecting—I mean, you don't normally visit—" I flushed, slammed the grate, and fumbled with the bar. I took a deep breath, then opened the door calmly, my head inclined slightly. "Welcome," I said.

My eyes darted up briefly to catch his smile, genuine as pure gold. Not mocking, as he should have done.

"Hello, Rae-Anna," he replied. He lifted the hand that held the sack mouth. "We had some surplus yestereve, and the council asked me to deliver it."

"They are very kind, as always," I said. It seemed strange to me that the village's "surplus" always seemed to be the same several loaves of oat bread, potatoes, turnips, and milled flour on the same several days of the week—almost as though it were planned—but I never said anything. Not to Thomas. "Please, come in," I offered, stepping back from the door as I inclined my head even further. Just in case anyone was watching.

He waited while I closed the oaken door again and led him toward our larder. "Are things well, in town?" I asked. I prayed nothing had occurred there like what had occurred to me an hour ago.

His silence worried me. I glanced back, and his gaze swung to mine quickly, his face pained. Forgetting myself, I stopped. "What is it?" I asked.

He reached out, nearly touching my arm, as he quickly shook his head. "Nothing. I'm fine. Keep walking. Please." I had never heard him like that, a pleading in his voice that somehow did not touch his eyes. But it was there.

I might not have hurried on if he seemed less upset. But somehow I knew it was most important to him. I continued on silently, as if we had never stopped. "Is your family well?" I asked after a moment.

"Very well, yes. Our Father's good providence has been on our fields, and my papa's health. We've had good crops, and we've been able to harvest all in time. Our lord is pleased."

"And your sister?" I asked. She had been courting for some months now.

I could feel the warmth of his smile before I glanced back to check. "Mama and Papa are pleased with her as well; hers is a good man. They will be wed in two weeks' time."

"So soon? And as late in the year?" Usually men waited to marry until fairer weather, and the promise of their own harvests surer.

"He has prenticed to the tailor, Pyotr." He must have caught the slight roll of my eyes, and he laughed. "Don't worry, the apprentice does not mirror the master. And Pyotr means no harm. He's…narrowly focused, that's all. Anyway, I'm told the prentice has a fine eye for it, and will do well. She'll see much more of the world than you or I."

A low buzz sounded in my ear, and I swatted at a fly I did not see or hit. I smiled at him, then stepped inside the kitchens. Sister Bethenny looked up from her pot. I smelled leeks and flour, and pepper? At least a little. She always was spare with the pepper. "The council has sent some surplus," I said as we made our way toward the larder.

She frowned and waved her hand firmly. "Don't put it in there, it won't keep. I'm sweeping it out before Lunens, but for now it's not safe. Rats," she finally explained. "That's why the soup." She rapped the spoon lightly against the kettle.

The image of that one rat, the one I barely saw but who seemed to see into me, flashed vividly to mind and I felt my face go pale as I gripped a finger. Sister Bethenny's frown deepened as she noticed.

"It is not that strange," she said, remembering herself as she slipped back into proper speech. "And Our Father's creatures do not mean us too much harm. But it forebodes a hard winter for us all if they seek our grain so soon. But Our Father provides regardless. Put the bags there, if you please." She pointed with the spoon to a low table against the wall, and Thomas dutifully deposited them. As he turned back he caught my eye, his question plain.

"Do you mind if I take a look?" I asked, turning to Sister Bethenny. "Just to see..." I could tell from her look she didn't approve.

"I looked quite closely, child," she began.

"I'm afraid I might have brought them in by accident," Thomas spoke up quickly. I raised an eyebrow at him, but he continued. "I brought some cheese last time—as a treat; I know your Mother Superior doesn't always approve, but...And you know how mice love cheese. If it's still in there, it should be removed. Or, if not," he hurried on, clearly recognizing as I did the impending 'no' in her opening mouth, "if it is gone, perhaps they will be, too, and you have little to fear."

She stared hard at both of us, and with fist on hip and swirling spoon said: "Leave the door open."

I ducked my head firmly and silently, flushing hard. I rushed down the short flight of stairs before any more words could be said and went deep into a far corner to look. I couldn't believe she had implied that! Well, I could believe it; most of the Sisters had thought I was here because I couldn't avoid such things. But I had forgotten Sister Bethenny still believed it, and she surprised me.

Thomas acted as though he were actually looking for the cheese, slowly making his way around the room and peering at the shelves. "I'm sorry," I said when he got close enough to hear a whisper.

He glanced at me quickly, then back at the shelves. "Why did the mention of rats shock you? You picked one up alive by its tail not three weeks ago and carried it outside as though you carried a radish."

I twisted my mouth. I had also forgotten I had done that. I wasn't sure why I did, then or now. It just seemed like something to do. Foolishness. But I couldn't help appreciating that he said it with a hint of awe, or at least admiration. It's nice to be admired, even if for foolishness.

But then my face fell again as I remembered his question. "Just something...strange. It happened just before you arrived. I got lost while I was making my prayers in the catacombs. And I came across some rats, or at least their footprints. It alarmed me; I didn't expect to find them there."

He stopped, hands on his hips, his gaze through the shelving now. The hinge of his jaw rippled and I knew he was piecing through what I hadn't said. "I don't think the cheese is in here anymore," he said. His eyes went to mine, briefly, and I could tell he read something there. Beloved Father, but he had a way about him! He looked, and he cared, and he...noticed. He noticed what was important, and not what was unimportant.

His gaze moved on as he continued to scan the shelves, while I scrambled to think of something else to say. "There was...music," I said finally, haltingly. "I've spoken to Sister Lucy about it. And she told me frightening things about some men who were monks here, a long time ago."

It was apparently Thomas' turn to go pale, though I saw it from behind. "What is it?" I asked quickly, forgetting to whisper.

He shook himself, his eyes continuing to search half-heartedly. "Garrett?" he asked, his whisper hoarse.

"Among several others, and him not the worst," I said slowly. "How do you know of them?"

"It's not unknown in the village," he said. "They were all originally from there. It's just a bad coincidence." He shook his head.

"What is? What happened?"

"Nothing *happened,* not really. Some travelers, journey-men-traders, staying overnight in town. I was in the pub—"

"Thomas..." I interrupted, intending to scold him. When he looked at me, I pressed my lips together briefly in apology. "Please, continue."

He drew a deep sigh. "I overheard some of their conversation with the publican. The one, the oldest it seemed to me, was descended from Garrett and was looking for his grave."

I took a step back, my hand rising involuntarily to my mouth.

"He got an earful, trust me," Thomas went on with a half-hearted smile. "The publican knew even more about it than I had ever heard." His shoulders shivered. "He assured them all in no uncertain terms that nothing good—and very much bad—was to be gained by seeking such a thing."

"Were they convinced?" I asked. It was, as he said, a bad coincidence, and one that nagged terribly.

"I had to go back out," Thomas said. "But anyone who wouldn't have been convinced..." He trailed off and swallowed, clearly not wanting to think about what kind of men wouldn't be dissuaded. He looked at me, the fear in his eyes I was sure mirroring my own. "I'm sure it'll be fine," he whispered.

"What will be fine?" a new voice demanded.

The shelves clattered as I backed against them, turning to see Sister Judith towering in the doorway. I quickly curtsied and kept my head bowed.

"Good even, Sister," Thomas said. "I was merely—"

"I was not asking you, young Thomas."

I swallowed in the silence. "There are some strange happenings in town, Sister..." I closed my eyes, already knowing I misspoke.

"You are not to concern yourself with happenings in town, are you," came the expected reply, with the expected harshness.

"No, Sister," I said. "There have been strange happenings here as well, though."

"Are they of concern to Thomas?"

I gritted my teeth, and shook my head. "I suppose not, Sister. Perhaps put together, though..." Her sharp sigh cut me off.

"Return to your cell," she said brusquely, inserting into the word every connotation it possessed. "And stay there in prayer until I come to you. Thomas, you will come to me and tell *me* of these...strange happenings. *I* will determine if they go together."

I felt Thomas stiffen beside me, and his voice when he spoke was tinged hoarse. "Yes, Sister."

I kept my eyes down as I scuttled past Sister Judith, glancing only briefly at Sister Bethenny's back; she, too, was bent with double earnestness to her task. Sister Judith had that effect, whether she spoke or no.

I glanced back only briefly as I entered my cell, leaving the door open. Thomas was following dutifully behind Sister Judith, his gaze firm upon the ground just behind her feet. Though I had seen one only once, he had the definite air of one headed to the gallows. I wasn't sure why. Too wrapped in my own despair, I didn't think on it for long. Instead I knelt beside my cot and fastened my eyes on the cross of our Beloved, pinned to the wall, and began my prayers.

I followed the form, at first. But, as always, I began to drift. I never told the Sisters I did; and, praise Our Father, I was able to keep to the forms when in their presence. But no matter what I tried, when on my own, I always left off and instead committed to mind everything I felt in my heart, sending it heavenward with all earnestness.

Tonight was worse than ever, though. I didn't even know what was in my heart—or, there was so much, I didn't know where to begin or end. The rats and strange men terrified me; the compulsion that had taken over my body overwhelmed me; the thought of staying in this place with those demons below undid me. I was desperate for protection, for wisdom, strength, independence. I didn't know if I wanted to know what was happening, or to wake up from some strange dream, or to simply turn and run back to the village. But I knew what waited for me there, too.

My head hurt from the thousand horses of thought stampeding through it; my stomach hurt from fear and lack of food; my knees hurt from the cold stone floor, though that pain would fade eventually. As Sister Judith delayed longer and longer, I assumed food would not be mine tonight. I suppose I deserved it, after the liberties I had taken.

"Have you been here the whole time?"

I let out a startled yelp, falling from my knees to a seated position. I faintly hated the cowardly form I presented. But Sister Judith's imperious stare took all my attention. I scuttled back to my knees, head bowing. "Yes, Sister; as directed."

She snorted her disbelief. "Easy to say," she said. I offered no proofs. There weren't any. "Well, take your seat," she continued finally. I glanced up, only then noticing the bowl in her hands. I rose despite my knees' protests, and sat demurely on the cot. She set the bowl on my lap before taking a seat opposite me. Without thinking, I picked up the spoon and scooped some of the cooled broth to my lips.

Despite the lack of seasoning, the leeks alone grasped my tongue and sent joy into my thoughts. Perhaps it was the breaking of my enforced fast. I ate a few more bites before the ominous silence broke through, and the spoonful in my mouth turned especially cold.

Sister Judith sat scandalized before me, her face hot and throttled as I knew she tried to think through how to punish me. "I-I'm sorry, Sister," I said, trying to quickly switch the spoon to my right hand.

I needn't have worried about spilling the broth as I tried to make the exchange. Sister Judith's wizened hand flew through the intervening space, and the bowl sounded as though it cracked as it bounced across the cloister and into the garden.

"Demon witch!" she seethed. "You did bring the rats and the ghosts, didn't you? I pray Our Father every day to take you from us! It is surely because of you we are cursed, for you bring your curse with you. No doubt indeed those men Thomas spoke of will arrive here before long, drawn by your evil and power!"

I didn't know how to reply. It was what I had been told since I could remember. Cursed with left-handedness, they said. And a beauty I could not deform or hide, enrapturing first boys, then men into temptation and sin. It seemed proper that I would bring disaster upon these Sisters who had tried to show me kindness. But I had nowhere else to go.

"I'm trying," I whispered. "I'm trying to be better," I amended quickly as Sister Judith's eyes goggled. "I pray every chance I get. I don't know why..." I trailed off as the thoughts threatened to overwhelm me again.

Sister Judith harrumphed. "Well, I know why. Perhaps it is not your fault; Our Father has mercy on whom He wills. But He hates those He hates, as well."

The fly returned, buzzing even closer this time, but I made no move to swat it. It would be a reminder to me that I was cursed, that I must always work to be better. Perhaps, if I spent all my strength in devotion, Our Father might relent and have mercy on me. And, if He chose not to, well...His will be done.

Sister Judith rose, and snatched the spoon from my hand. "Perhaps another night in prayer," she said. Her tone told me clearly she didn't believe it.

She left, and I returned to my knees. It was a position I had come to value, in its own way.

Chapter 3

I awoke slumped against the bed. Someone—presumably not Sister Judith—had covered my shoulders with a blanket, and had closed the door to my cell. A bright sky peeped in through the iron lattice window near the top of the door. I had heard no bells, though perhaps their tolling away was what had woken me.

My eyes went automatically to the image of The Beloved, whose head still bowed toward mine in pity. Or shame. Normally his head was turned slightly away, but this morning from my awkward position it seemed more like he bent toward me. I took some small comfort in that.

I arose painfully on stiff joints, and after a groan and mumble threw the blanket over the cot and pulled it tight. There was a rough clay cup of water on my small table, which I hurriedly drank. It reminded me of how long ago I had eaten, and how little it had been. I wondered if I was permitted to take some food.

I opened the door. The small window had given me a false impression: the garden was still dark, the sky mostly overcast with thick clouds. It had been only one small opening that seemed so bright. I shivered, hugging myself. Not the morning I hoped to wake up to.

A breeze was stirring, and the rope to the bell tower swayed. There would be strength behind that wind by time the sun rose enough to gloom the convent through the gray. I shuffled on bare feet over cold flagstones toward the kitchen. We were not permitted to put on shoes of any kind after penance until commanded.

I smelled the bread long before I reached Sister Bethenny's domains, warm and yeasty and nutty. She was probably trying to use up more of our stores to keep it from the rats. There was no other reason to be so generous with the ingredients.

The scent alone was almost enough to satisfy me. I made my presence known with a small scrape of my foot, scuffing as I stepped through the archway. The oven blazed, heating the room, and now I smelled her sweat mingling with the bread. She cast an arched eyebrow my direction and compressed her lips. After a pause, she looked pointedly toward a cloth-wrapped bundle, and turned silently back to her baking. Though she wouldn't see it, I still bowed my head in thanks. I hugged the bundle tightly to my chest, letting the warmth soak through it and my dress and into my skin as I moved back to my cell.

I sat on my cot and broke the bread, sparing a prayer for The Beloved's body broken for the Sisters. I paused, watching the steam curl up from the crumbled brown halves flecked with walnuts. Mother Superior had read to us, once, about The Beloved praying for those who had tortured and hung him to die. He prayed God's mercy over them, she read—that they didn't know what they were doing. I did not know what I was doing either, except trying my best. Why wouldn't he pray for mercy on me, too?

Maybe he did. But it didn't matter for one who was cursed. I bit into the bread. I knew it wasn't true Fellowship—that could only be administered by Mother Superior, and not for me until I was a Sister—but it felt more refreshing and life-giving than a normal piece of bread. But then, The Liar tempted The Beloved with bread too, once. I swallowed hard, waiting for it to turn to ash in my mouth—at least, I assumed that's what it would do. The Liar's promises quickly turned hollow, I was taught. But it still felt like bread, and I took another bite.

The bells rang Gemmans, and I looked up. The Sisters were shuffling by. I re-wrapped the loaf and placed it on my table, then turned for the door. Sister Lucy was looking at me. "Put shoes on, and come to the chapel," she said. Before I could thank her, she turned and left.

It could be confusing, when the other Sisters treated me with kindness and mercy, while the eldest and Superior-in-Waiting seemed far more concerned with my sanctification than they. At least, Sister Judith spent far more time speaking of the strait road I had yet to follow than they did.

But I would make myself late in pondering. I slipped my feet into the rough shoes and stepped into the cloister, moving quietly and purposefully toward the chapel where the last Sister's robes swirled through the door.

I entered quickly but quietly as the last toll's echo faded away. I had been to the church inside the village a few times before coming to the convent, had marveled at the colored glass windows and high vaulted ceilings. The Sisters—and presumably the Brothers before them—considered all that a distraction. No ceiling could replace Our Father's own vault of sky, no colored glass should mimic the colors of sunrise, rainbow, or autumn. I couldn't fault them for this, and yet the austerity of the little chapel reminded me more of just another prison than Our Father's glorious creation. And on weary days like today, it was that much worse.

I slid across the back wall, taking my appropriate kneeling position in the far corner. Sister Judith spared me no glance, but I could tell from the change in her posture that she marked my presence. She always did, and many other Sisters did as well. I wasn't sure if it was a comfort or not: they struggled with allowing one supposedly cursed into the chapel, just as much as I did. Normally, that curse would have to be resolved before I would be granted entrance—at least, so Sister Judith told me. The other Sisters' discomfort told me they knew the same. Only the more obvious fact that I did not burn alive or drop dead stood as proof against it. But I couldn't help but wonder if Our Father was just waiting for a more opportune time, and so I took my life in my hands every time I came in. I was ashamed to admit sometimes I entered quietly so as to not provoke Our Father's attention. Maybe if I made no noise, He would not remember I was there, and judgment that was supposed to come would be delayed another day.

Of course I knew that was silly. To the extent I prayed while I was there—which I did, most fervently—His attention would be drawn whether I was invisible or came in bashing a great pair of bells. Oddly, that desire came over me sometimes as well, to make a great noise upon entering. Mother Superior had read just the day before her journey that we should enter His courts with praise. I stole in like a thief.

Sister Judith was chanting in a jarringly melodious voice. I could never reconcile her severity with her voice, like a pig in silk. I swallowed, quickly asking forgiveness for such an unpleasant thought. I took the opportunity to continue in more prayer, while keeping one ear on the chant. It worked a miracle, I had to admit. Behind closed eyes I could transport myself to a field of flowers, the sky bright overhead. As she continued, the sky darkened. Clouds swept in and the land grew dark. The flowers shriveled and returned to the ground. I was inside an ancient city, atop a bald hill. Suddenly, The Beloved was before me, hung and bleeding between the thieves. I nearly gasped; he was torn and ragged far beyond any image or representation I had seen. I turned my eyes away; he was entirely naked. Always in images or on pages the artist left him with some glory, some vestige of honor or dignity. That despite the circumstances, it was still his choice and under his power to stay or go—and thus, he retained some bearing of a king, of a man in full control.

This is not what I saw in this vision brought on by Sister Judith's chant, and of course I wondered if it were actually from her or not. Instead, before me was someone no one would admire. Here hung someone utterly cursed and broken, abandoned, on display as one sucked completely hollow of dignity, self-worth, importance. His suffering was not even noteworthy. Those who gathered were only those who knew him personally, or were there because they had to be. It was not even a spectacle worth a crowd. If any others were there, it was by happenstance.

I knew that was not how the story ended. In fact, in a few short moments several things would happen that would draw the attention of millions down through the ages. But right now, in the moment of my vision, that had not happened yet. And those gathered did not know it would be any different. This moment had moved beyond the piteous and had entered the ridiculous. All of his grand speeches and radical ways were made as hollow as his spirit. He was no one special, had only fooled them for a time, and now died worse than any wicked or unimportant man.

The sky darkened to near blackness, and to me it stopped being a vision and became reality. The stone of the chapel beneath my knees became the stone of that Sacred Mount. The air around me reeked with his blood. I sensed rather than saw the spear entering his side.

But when the ground convulsed at his departing spirit, several of the Sisters shrieked, and Sister Judith's chant died abruptly. I opened my eyes as thunder crashed outside. The rest glanced in fear at each other; Sister Judith looked straight at me. I looked at myself, expecting fire or skin blackened by lightning. To my shock, and soon horror, I appeared to myself healthier and more vital than I ever had. I cannot—will not—say my clothes shined. That would be too much. But they certainly appeared new. I gulped, running a hand down my front. A corner of my mind asked wryly if I was hoping to re-soil myself, to make dingy the cleanliness I seemed to have acquired. A separate corner thought this was the obvious solution. I did, after all, run my left hand down my dress.

Another roll of thunder, this time more distant. It seemed to be a normal, natural thunderstorm. Nevertheless, we all went outside to see what—if any—damage had occurred from the strange tremor.

The garden looked as it had, under brooding skies and sheeting rain. The Sisters whispered among themselves, drawing their whipping cloaks tighter. In my simple dress, I had nothing to gather, and only stood and looked. Here and there, I began to notice bits of stone or debris. But otherwise, all seemed intact. Our gates remained fast, the small towers unmoved.

"Did you do this?" Sister Judith asked of me.

Sister Lucy's head turned swiftly. "Do what, create a storm?"

"You know what I mean," she snapped back, her furious gaze withdrawn for a moment.

Sister Lucy continued to stare at her as though she were simple. "How would she have anything to do with an earthquake? She is powerful indeed if she can pray up something like that. Perhaps we should ask her to pray for the conversion of the whole village, if Our Father answers her so mightily."

"I do not think it would be The Father who would be answering her," Sister Judith seethed. "It is not as if strange things have not happened to her, and recently."

Sister Lucy looked at me patiently. "Child, did you ask for a tremor? I saw you deep in prayer."

"I..." The words died on my lips. It sounded strange in my head; it would not sound right coming out of my mouth. Not in front of Sister Judith. But they waited an answer. "No, Sisters. I was contemplating The Beloved's sacrifice. Sister Judith's chant brought it clearly to my mind."

"I imagine the tremor coincided with the quake that brought the Captain to repentance," Sister Lucy said wryly.

I swallowed hard. Fortunately Sister Judith was busy giving Sister Lucy a withering look, who was better at keeping her face calm than I was. Still, I could tell Sister Lucy noticed, and her glance told me we would speak later.

Another bolt brilliantly lit the garden, and I shuddered. I couldn't explain it, and surely didn't want to try, but something still felt strange. The vision had felt more real than anything I had experienced before, and now there was a tension in the air. Not because Sister Judith stood there thinking I somehow caused an earthquake; that, from her, didn't surprise me anymore. But there was a menace in the air, like seeing some vast stone teetering on a cliff while someone walks below. I just didn't know how to call out a warning, or if I even needed to.

"Sisters, go quickly to your stations and check on them each," Sister Judith said. "Sister Lucy, when you have checked our stores, look also at those rooms we do not use—the dormitories and former brewhouse."

I stood silently by, waiting my instructions. I assumed they would include the cell. Sister Judith turned to me and stared for some moments. "You as well, child; go to your responsibilities."

I didn't think she could mean what she meant, and so I only stared back. Finally she gave me a grim smile. "Sister Lucy thinks you are to be trusted. Let us test you, then. Check on the catacombs, and make sure there have been no cave-ins."

"Sister Judith, do you think that wise?" Sister Lucy asked. She had been about to leave with the other Sisters, but paused now.

"No," Sister Judith said frankly, her eyes still boring into me. "But none here seem ready to heed my wisdom, so I will join in their folly. Go," she said firmly to me. By the power of her voice alone I turned and left.

I strode along the cloister, flinching as another nearby bolt threw puddles in ghastly white light. The trees of the garden, lifeless enough with their leaves gone and bare branches like bones, were positively menacing as they appeared suddenly in the clouded darkness with arms waving as though to grab passersby and throw them over the walls. I passed through the sacristy, now empty—none had yet taken the time to return the items from the chapel. Instead of a cleansing, I felt the menace grow stronger. I took one of the rushlights that lined the wall and held it to the thick candle that burned perpetually at the entrance. It flared to life, and I tucked it into a lantern. The storm still raged outside, but in the quiet of the sacristy I paused to offer another few prayers. It felt good to be sheltered by stone again.

I stared at the door to the catacombs ahead of me. It looked the same in the dim light, but I considered briefly going only barely inside and hiding until it seemed appropriate, then coming back out and telling Sister Judith everything was fine. But only briefly. I did still want to take my place in the convent, and being discovered in a lie would end that hope. And it would prove Sister Judith right. It was probably that thought more than any other that pushed me through the door and down the stairs beyond.

Everything did seem fine, at first. And though the walls and ceiling all seemed sound, the deeper I went the more a buzzing grew in my ear. I thought somehow the fly had followed me. But it was more incessant and more...predatory, it seemed. Besides the fact no fly would have been out in the storm.

I found myself at the turn once more where the dust and rat prints began, and my footprints from yesterday. The buzzing was a whine now, and faintly below it I thought I heard strange voices, as though it had been a chant all along.

I had inspected my area of responsibility. There was absolutely no reason to go on. As strange as the events yesterday had been, the whine and voices now marked it even stranger. I should have run.

Except, perhaps, I should not have.

Debating doesn't matter; I did not turn back, but kept going. After a turn or two, a faint blue light began to tinge the walls ahead of me as though the stones reflected some far-off glow. The whine grew until it reached such a pitch that I could no longer hear it. The voices babbled incoherently. I noticed, through an almost overpowering urge to continue, that some voices seemed dark and violent while others were pleading, and still others were calm and reassuring. The blue light grew.

Suddenly, I heard another great roll of thunder. I stopped. I had forgotten the storm in the quiet of the catacombs, and now wondered how I could hear it again. The voices dimmed beneath a patter of rain, though the glow remained strong. The orange of my rushlight danced, and I looked at a flame bucking as if in a strong breeze, though I felt nothing on my face.

Finally I began to walk forward again. I knew, in some corner of my mind, I was near the alcoves of the damned monks. I feared what I would find, but knew I had to find it. With a deep breath I rounded another turn.

The ceiling here had caved in, and rain came through the opening. Lightning flashed above and thunder rumbled down, but that was not the source of the light. The markers on the alcoves, those dread memories of these terrible men, were slicked with rain. The writing, which before had been worn with age, was stark and clean as though newly-carved. And around each was a halo of dancing blue flame untouched by rain or wind.

I stared. As before, my legs were not mine to command. I shuffled forward, drawn to this strange fire. The voices now babbled at me as though coming from every tomb, but I still could not separate one from another.

The fire fascinated me. I could feel no heat as I drew near, and though it danced the light it emitted was steady. I found myself reaching out my hand. I don't know why. But it seemed somehow right.

For a moment I paused, wondering. But then I plunged my left hand directly into the flames. Frozen in horror I watched as the fire rushed into my hand, running from the stones like rats converging on a morsel and disappearing into my flesh.

The blue fire went out. My rushlight went out. And I felt myself falling backward as darkness surrounded me.

Chapter 4

When I awoke, I was staring at the ceiling of my cell. The rain had ceased. The light was orange from a candle. I pulled my hands from beneath the coarse wool blanket and looked at them. They were not burned. I couldn't say I felt differently—perhaps better-rested. And I wasn't hungry. If it was night time again, I thought I should be.

Ye shall not live by bread alone.

Mother Superior had said it often enough, as had Sister Judith though more harshly. Though I had not eaten well in the village, it oftentimes felt like I ate better there than here. And so I had to be reminded of those words a lot the first month or so. Perhaps I had finally gotten used to it.

I raised my head. The cell was empty, and the small grate on the door was indeed black. But had it been only one day? I thought a Sister should be here, watching over me until I awoke. Surely one of them had brought me here—and just left me, unconscious?

Maybe she had only stepped out. Or maybe Sister Judith found me,

brought me up, and left me to die or live. There was no way to know
until one of them came back.

Or should I get up? I contemplated for several breaths, then
levered myself up to a sitting position. I felt fine—odd, I thought,
for having had blue fire invade me. I still didn't know what to make
of that, or any of it. I let my thoughts drift, to see if they would
tend toward something vile. I found myself turning to look at The
Beloved. The same sense of compassion washed over me that I had
felt during the vision. I thought it should be disgust or hatred, if I
had become evil.

Absently I scratched my hand at a faint itch, as though tickled
by a hair. My mind continued to drift, back to the catacombs. Why
had it caved in? That had not been clear in the brief moments I was
there. The earth above seemed thick, and I had some sense of how
deep it must be—there were several sets of stairs downward. And the
catacombs were arched with brick. The hole, what I could remember,
was small, more as though someone had dug down, than the earth
itself had collapsed. Could it have been the men Thomas spoke of?
Did they somehow know where the crypts would be, and tried to find
it?

I scratched again. The itch wouldn't go away. I vaguely registered
the blue glint on The Beloved just as I glanced down at my hands to
see what tickled me.

I shrieked. The fire was back, surrounding my fingers in a nimbus.
I shook my hand vigorously as though it was actually on fire. It was
reflex. But I still felt no heat, and shaking it did not extinguish the
flame. I put the hand under the blanket to smother it, but when I
removed it the flames returned.

I panted. What was happening to me? What was it? Where was it
from?

I will not leave you comfortless: I will come to you.

I stared at the flames. Were they speaking to me? Or at least in me? The moments passed. Who are you?

Ye know me; for I dwelleth with you and shall be in you.

Should I be afraid of you? Are you...evil?

The world cannot receive me, because it seeth me not, neither knoweth me.

But...what are you? Why are you here? What's happening to me?

Because he lives, ye shall live also.

That doesn't help me! Please just answer my questions—the ones I actually ask.

The fire went out. I stared hard at my hand, trying to will the fire back. There was silence, inside and outside. I let my hand fall. Odd, how quickly I went from trying to put the flames out, to wishing them back. But I knew they were something separate from me, and yet a part of me. I just wish they had answered me more clearly.

But, then, they had given some words of comfort: I would live. They were not set to harm me, or to lead me to harm—at least, not to death. And though I didn't know what it was right now, they did say I knew them because they lived in me. Wasn't that a promise that it was something knowable?

I startled as I heard a knocking on the door. I sat stunned for a moment. Why would one of the Sisters knock? Usually they simply entered. Then I wondered that the fire had gone out mere seconds before she arrived.

"Come...in?" I said tentatively.

Instead, more knocking. It didn't sound like knuckles, I realized. I furrowed my brow. "Who's there?" I called out. "I'm awake. You can come in."

I heard low voices outside, but couldn't make out their speech. I stood and went to the door, bent my ear to listen. But it was still muffled. I peered through the grate; impenetrable darkness was on the other side. "Hello?" I called. The voices continued as though I had not spoken.

Thoroughly perplexed, I turned around—and shrieked again. I hated how much I was doing that, lately. I couldn't help it. I saw myself still stretched out upon the cot as though asleep. The light from the candle hovered like a bubble around the flame, reaching no further than my hands clasped on my chest. The rest of the room was in darkness. I couldn't tell if it was empty or not. But I had seen it was empty when I awoke—or had I still dreamed? But the fire and the voice seemed so real. And I was hearing knocking and voices.

Why would they knock on the door of someone sleeping?

How did I wake myself up? Perhaps I was on the verge, which was how I heard voices but not what they said. I reached behind me and felt for the door; though resistance met my hand, I couldn't feel the rough planking. I must somehow be dreaming.

Unless I was already dead.

Because he lives, ye shall live also, the fire had said. Or was it actually the fire? Or just a dream? Would a promise made in a dream still come true?

I stomped my foot, beat my hands against my thighs, pinched the backside of my arm. I felt none of it. My panic started rising again. Was I stuck like this forever?

I turned and tried to open the door. The latch rattled, clicked open, but the door itself refused to swing outward. I turned back, staring at myself, trying to will myself awake. I swung my fist backward to thump the door—and saw that same arm twitch under the blanket.

I squinted, then stomped a foot. The same foot twitched. I screamed; in bed, I moaned. My breathing slowed, and I walked forward, watching my head shift minutely on the sweat-drenched napkin.

I didn't know why, but I sat down on the bed. After a glance back and forth, I lay down, trying to align myself with my sleeping form. I still felt nothing. I closed my eyes and prayed.

The voices grew louder, more distinct. I blinked my eyes open. The only light was from a candle. I could feel the rough wool blanket over me. How did I get here? My thoughts were fuzzy, but slowly I remembered the blue fire and some strange dream.

"She's awake," I heard suddenly. I turned my head, and Sister Lucy was peering at me.

"How do you feel?" she asked, her voice wary.

My tongue was dry, and stuck to my mouth, so all I could manage was "Mnine" and to move my jaw a few times. Sister Jenneth, our gardener and healer, stood beside her and looked at me with the same distaste and wariness as I had seen her look at rats and bugs.

Sister Lucy *humphed* and drew closer. "Can you sit up?"

As I tried, she lifted a small cup from the table and held it patiently. It took me a few moments until I was sitting awkwardly. I did feel mostly fine, just tired and my limbs wouldn't do exactly what I asked. Finally she held out the cup. I stared at it, waiting for my hand to take it from her.

Finally she clucked and held the rim to my lips. Sister Jenneth made some sort of protest, but I was too busy swallowing the cool liquid to pay attention.

"Well, we need to know what happened before we need to be afraid of her," Sister Lucy replied.

I finished swallowing and let myself collapse against the wall. I thought they should be afraid of me. But something in the dream—a feeling I couldn't express—told me they shouldn't.

"Do you remember what happened?" Sister Lucy pressed.

"Some, Sister," I said. "Though, not when..."

"We went to look for you at next bells," she replied. "I thought the catacombs shouldn't take you so long, but you are so often thorough." Though her voice was dry, I felt she meant it honestly. "But, in truth, I feared for you. I thought you would be smarter. Until I saw the second set of footprints." Her lips compressed, and I knew she waited for explanation.

"I'm sorry, Sister," I said. "I don't know what—something compelled me..." I trailed off, knowing what that might sound like. "Not—it didn't force me, not at first. But everything has been so strange, I thought I had to check...as you said, be thorough."

Sister Lucy glanced sideways, a mixed look of triumph and yet of fear.

"Not at first?" Sister Jenneth asked.

"Well, once I got to the tombs, and saw the fire—" I cut off as both gazes bored into me.

"What fire?" they asked, almost in unison.

I sagged further. "The markers were limned in blue flame," I said. I couldn't make myself say the rest. In the silence, Sister Lucy took a cautious step forward; Sister Jenneth edged toward the door.

"What happened then?" Sister Lucy asked.

"I went forward. The light from the flames were steady, and they weren't hot—they just...were. I thought about the story—the fire that didn't consume the bush—and so I reached out my hand." Again I paused, not wanting to tell them it had rushed into my hand and disappeared. "And then...and then I fainted, I think."

As though on command, Sister Jenneth fainted. Sister Lucy gasped and stepped backward, drawing the Holy Symbol in the air before her. I felt the itch before I even looked, and wanted to weep. The blue fire was in my hand, and I could tell it chided me.

"The fire came into me," I said hurriedly, eager to get the truth out. "I don't know why or what it is..."

But Sister Lucy wasn't listening. She grabbed Sister Jenneth by the back of her cloak and dragged her limp form through the door. I heard the thump of her hitting the stone walk of the cloister, and the door banged shut. There was another sound, one I had never heard on my door, of metal rattling.

"I don't think it means us harm!" I shouted, my wits finally returning. I stood shakily and moved to the door. "It hasn't done anything yet, anyway." Outside I heard dragging again, and Sister Lucy calling for help. A rush of footsteps. "Sisters, please!" I called out. "Help me!"

I tried to open the door, but though the latch rattled the door was stuck. I whirled again, but my bed was empty. This was no dream. "What are you going to do?" I called out. I wasn't sure if they could hear me above the tumult that I assumed surrounded the two Sisters as Lucy tried to explain. There were too many raised voices for me to hear, until finally Sister Judith's rang loud and clear.

"Enough!" The cacophony ended abruptly. "Get her to her room and give her cool water, and whatever else she requires. Is the other one secure?" I couldn't hear the response. "Very well. No one goes near it until we've met about this. Did she harm anyone directly? Or does she seem harmed?"

The response, once more, was too low for me to hear, and the rest of the conversation followed suit. I trembled, fearing Sister Judith. Even if she had never been looking for a reason to throw me from the convent, she had one now. But I knew she *had* been looking for a reason—had come up with several.

There was another commotion, which I interpreted as several of the Sisters carrying Sister Jenneth away. I put my forehead against the door, whispering what prayers I could think of.

"Cease that babbling," came harshly from the other side of the door. I gasped, and stepped back.

"Sister Judith, please—"

"Silence, now, and listen: you leave us no choice. It is well you have not caused harm yet, but not well enough. You should be gone tonight, but unfortunately we must do things properly against the Mother Superior's return. For all we know, she favors you..." Her voice trailed off into bitterness. After a moment, it returned, cold and hard. "The best you can do right now is be silent, and prepare yourself for life outside the walls of this convent again. Though who will take you in..."

In the suggestive silence, a small flame flickered on the tip of my finger. I stared at it angrily, wishing with sheer force of will that I could make it leave.

I defend the poor and fatherless, and do justice to the afflicted and needy. The flame winked out.

"Stay here, and stay silent," Sister Judith continued. As if I could leave, or they would hear me once they left the cloister. "Someone will come for you before the end of the night."

Her footsteps receded, and I turned and sat on my bed. I drew a deep sigh and looked at my hands, trying not to wish the flame to return, to give me some other comfort than what it already had. So far, aside from frightening me almost senseless by its presence alone, that was all it had done: speak words of wisdom and comfort in my mind. And something about the words seemed familiar, though I didn't know why.

I lost track of time until the bells began to ring Scuros—dinner-time. I thought back; we had gone to inspect our areas just after dawn. I had slept through three prayer times, at least. My stomach was not so hollow as to feel like I had been senseless for an entire day or more. I wondered how much longer they would leave me in here without food.

Outside I heard faint footfalls as the Sisters went to Chapel to pray. I arrayed myself, waiting for the clanking iron at the door. It never came. The echo of the bells rolled away, the last footsteps finally receded, and all was silent. My cell was far enough away I wouldn't hear the chanting.

I leaned back, looking probably as desperate as I felt with my body slumped and my head pushed forward hard by the wall behind my cot, below The Beloved. As the minutes dragged on, I found it harder and harder to care. I had fought and struggled against my curses from the day I had arrived at the convent. I had considered self-mutilation for the one—no man would be attracted to a scarred face. There were not enough meals to gain weight, to hope to hide behind rolls of fat; I thought perhaps if I became sickly, it might help as well. But Mother Superior, when she noticed, compelled me to eat more. I could not help the Sisters, she said, without the strength to do my tasks. I did not put much stock in that 'curse' anyway—not enough to truly commit. Most men who leered set low standards, and even those whose advances were subtler cared mostly that I was young and female. I suspected little else mattered, and no amount of roughness or dress would lessen the looks or calls.

As for the other, I had learned to do almost everything with my right hand. I would never be a scribe, but I was a passable seamstress and could do well at weaving. When they let me. So far, though, they seemed to prefer cleaning tasks for me. With any of those three, though, I thought I might do well enough in the world. And far easier, I thought, than the constant wariness and distrust from most of the Sisters. Even with several months of practice, I still used my left hand when I wasn't thinking, or when surprised. Maybe with more practice, but from how many positions would I be turned out before I could build the habit? Would I be beggared by then?

Perhaps most frustrating was that it was not my choice. To leave, was; Sister Judith was quite plainly happy with my ability to leave. Any other acolyte spent her first year *deciding* if she wanted to stay; I had spent my first year so far *fighting* for that possibility. The rankling of that distinction probably kept me there longer than if I was able—personally—to simply give up. Such an attitude seemed beyond my personality though. I needed to prove I was not cursed.

Despite my awkward position, with my chin digging into my chest, I must have dozed. I didn't hear the lock opening, and became aware only as Sister Lucy stepped across the threshold. She paused and stared at me with an expression I couldn't read. I wished she would just tell me to leave, or something. I sat up, but couldn't continue to look her in the eye.

"Has this fire harmed you?" she asked. I shook my head. "Has it done anything besides appear occasionally?"

I thought about the words it seemed to speak, but I couldn't be sure that was the fire or something else. Except, I assumed it was the fire. I knew I should tell her, mostly because I was afraid it would appear again if I tried to lie.

But before I could speak, she seemed to take my silence for a 'no.' "Does it come or go to your bidding? Can you control it?" I shook my head again. There was a pause. "I want to be very clear on this, child, so I need you to look at me." I obeyed. Her eyes were earnest, but also held a hint of the kindness I had come to appreciate. "Child, would you be rid of this thing, if it were your will? Did you do anything outside of innocent curiosity to cause it to come into you?"

"I did not, Sister, I swear it. I don't know what it is, why it's in me. I would be rid of it only because I fear harming anyone here."

She must have seen my earnestness, because she relaxed visibly. "Then I am happy to tell you we have prevailed against Sister Judith. No," she said quickly, holding up a hand as my mouth opened. "I won't tell you who precisely. It is not important, nor should your respect or obedience to Sister Judith diminish in the slightest. This is a—well, what men call a stay of execution. We will do what is in our power and knowledge to eradicate this fire from you until Mother Superior returns. If it remains, she will judge what to do with you."

My first thoughts were joy and gratitude. In truth, I wanted desperately to stay. But some small corner of me still struggled with the idea that it was not up to me, and that corner sulked. I let none of that out, though I worried that some sign of it crossed my face.

I bowed my head again, in humility and to be sure to hide anything I wished hidden. "What must I do, Sister?" I asked, truly humble. I did want it gone. I did.

"First," Sister Lucy said, and I could hear the warmth in her voice. "You must eat."

Chapter 5

I stood barefoot in a coarse wool gown before the Sisters in our Chapterhouse. Head bowed, I kept my hands clasped behind me as Sister Judith led a long prayer about sin and confession. Finally she paused. I dared not look up.

"Child Rae-Anna, kneel and clasp your hands before you," she said. I obeyed. Then, beginning with the Sister furthest from Judith, they each in turn began to denounce the fire that had come to me. Sister Jenneth proclaimed the goodness of Our Father's creation, the righteousness of each part acting in its place, the folly and evil in any part acting out of place. Sister Bethenny similarly extolled the virtues of fire for warmth and baking and roasting (though we should not put much effort into getting those, only what Our Father graciously provided), then warned sternly of the dangers of fire escaped from the hearth. Sister Lucy was perhaps most gracious, not calling out the fire specifically, but her intention in this setting could not be mistaken. Sister Aitrinn, who kept our livestock, spoke of the good sense her animals had in the presence of fire, and that others would do well to learn from their caution.

As they went, I felt an ire growing in me that I couldn't explain. The words they spoke made sense, and yet I felt an inexplicable anger at their attitude. I thought perhaps because I felt blameless—it was not as though I asked for this fire. But it soon seemed separate from me. It was as Sister Aitrinn spoke that it occurred to me: this was clearly not ordinary fire. The fire that "dumb" animals feared actually had the power to burn, and to kill. So far this fire had done neither. Ordinary fire spread if not controlled—Sister Bethenny made that clear. And yet the fire in me had not once gone beyond my hands, though I was also clearly in no control over it. It had, from the moment I saw it, governed itself as no ordinary fire would. It did not burn me, it did not burn my blanket or my clothes when I held my hands in my lap and the flames danced without me seeing.

So here were these several Sisters, so learned in our world, treating and denouncing something utterly abnormal as though it were normal. I wanted the fire gone, I knew. But this did not seem the way to go about it.

In truth, a bit of pride pricked me as well, at the suggestion that I was stupider than an ox to reach my hand into a flame that didn't burn me. Oxen are stupid because they aren't curious. Hang me that I was.

Finally it was Sister Judith's turn. I was well to fear her words, because she would also pronounce their judgment and sentencing.

"We find this fire to be wholly strange, and likely of great evil," she began, her voice the thunder of doom. "It was born, to our knowledge, upon the sepulchers of men wholly devoted to the abominable Dragon, having given him multitudinous and heinous sacrifices in a lust for power." That was true enough, I had to admit. "Their punishments were well-earned, and perhaps still lenient." Her strangled voice told me she thought I deserved the same. With this, I did not agree. "Such fire cannot be permitted to remain within these sacred walls." Again, her tone told me she wished me gone. I heard a faint cough from one of the other Sisters—I guessed Lucy; I loved her so dearly—and with a short sigh Sister Judith continued. "To this end, we have arranged a series of penances and tasks to try to eradicate this fire from the child Rae-Anna. First, she is to remain in her coarse wool until this fire has gone as a sign of her discomfort—her *extreme discomfort*—at having this fire within her. Second, she is barred from the catacombs indefinitely; her duty will be in the scullery and the many deep corners of our convent where the Sisters can not often make it, cleaning dust and cobwebs and darkness from every inch. As she does this she will strive to similarly go into every corner of her being to find also the dust and cobwebs of sin that still remain, that by the cleansing of those corners she may be righteous. Third, she will be given the barest amount of food, living instead off the words of Our Father, that by those words also she may find righteousness. Fourth, at every moment she is not engaged in her tasks, she will kneel before The Beloved in earnest prayer that this fire be removed. Finally, she will be fitted with a bell around her neck so we can determine her movements, that she not come in contact with any Sister until this fire is gone. Does any Sister have anything to add?"

No contact with any Sister, not even Lucy. I did not know what I would do without her encouragement and care. In the horrified silence, I heard only a faint shifting—one, I felt, indicating discomfort. They were not all happy with these stipulations. But I imagined Sister Judith offered them the choice between these or my banishment from the convent, and they agreed to the former. It still staggered me how one so severe held so much power. I wondered how she got it.

"Does the child wish to add anything, beyond thankfulness for our mercy?" Sister Judith asked, her voice thick with scorn.

I confess, if the anger had not been stirred in me, I would probably have kept silent. But despite this trembling rage, I kept my voice as meek as I could—because, I did truly want to know. "If I may not be in contact with any of the Sisters, how will you know the fire is gone?"

A rustling swept through the Sisters, and one of them coughed loudly—it seemed to me to hide a laugh, but that may have been my own interpretation. When silence again descended, Sister Judith spoke coldly.

"Very well. A watch will be posted by your cell whenever you are in it, to see if flames are ever observed. And of course you, *child,* will be sure to report to that watch any observance by you of this fire. Will that suffice us all?"

There was a general murmur of agreement, then silence again. I knew she emphasized *child* to remind me they were no nearer to considering me a daughter—an acolyte deemed worthy of Sisterhood who lacked only the vows. I knew others who had earned this distinction after as many months, and the complete silence told me it was not only Sister Judith who felt this way. I startled as that silence was shattered by the loud clanging of a bell as it crashed to the floor in front of me.

"Put it on," Sister Judith said, her voice utterly contemptuous. "If it is determined that you fail in any of these five stipulations—by intention or by accident—you will be banished from these walls forever." She waited while I picked up the bell and secured it firmly around my neck by the little leather thong attached to it. It hung heavy, and I felt the cord bite into my skin. "First report to the scullery; there is much work to do there. When you have finished, go to the dormitories and clean until too dark to do so. When you report to your cell, you will find your ration, and a schedule to keep until Mother Superior returns. Now go."

I bowed my head a little deeper, and turned as I rose. I walked out without looking at any of them. As soon as I entered the cloister on my way to the scullery, the blue flames came to my hands.

The world cannot receive me, because it seeth me not, neither knoweth me.

But Sister Judith is not of the world; she is The Beloved's.

Not every one that saith, Lord, Lord, shall enter into the kingdom; but he that doeth the will of Our Father.

Isn't she doing His will? She seems most devout.

Ye shall not afflict any widow, or fatherless child. If thou afflict them in any wise, and they cry at all unto me, I will surely hear their cry; and my wrath shall wax hot.

The flame winked out. Though Sister Judith's hatred of me—I did not even want to say hatred; her seemingly unfair and harsh treatment of me—felt oppressive, I feared for her as those words echoed through me. I didn't know why, or what would happen, but I knew that her judgement was as surely pronounced as mine, though not as publicly. As though she were already on her way to the gallows where the noose hung stark. And I found no joy in it.

That first evening did not go as badly as I feared. I lay into each task earnestly—though I quickly had to learn ways to work without the bell ringing and driving me mad. I did think about The Beloved and his sacrifice, and the washing away of my own sins. I enjoyed the quiet, found peace in the dripping water and *hish, hish, hish* of the scrubbing brush. As I wiped away sweat, I imagined it to be The Liar's pollution squeezing out of me. And I thought, perhaps, by morning the fire would be gone.

That night I found a crusty half-loaf of bread and cup of water, and a stern-faced and silent Sister Jenneth sitting just outside the door. "The fire came to me after the judgement, but not since," I said. Her lips tightened, and it seemed she withdrew further though she did not actually move from her chair. I went inside my cell, quickly ate and drank, then knelt for prayers.

My back ached, in part from stooping over pots and pans and plates and bowls, and then over the stones of the floor as I scrubbed it clean. But it also now ached from the sense of Sister Jenneth's eyes boring into me. I didn't feel worthy of prayer. With this fire still in me (as far as I knew) what right had I to kneel before The Beloved?

Father, forgive them: for they know not what they do.

Sister Jenneth hissed behind me, and I clamped my hand under the thin sheet. It was back.

Please leave, I begged, near to tears.

What I do thou knowest not now; but thou shalt know hereafter.

Silence, except for one sob I couldn't suppress. I felt a shift in the air that I didn't understand, and didn't respond to. But suddenly I felt a presence very near me, and looked up at Sister Jenneth in surprise. Her hand was extended toward me, but still some distance away. In her eyes was suddenly compassion.

"I can tell you don't want this," she whispered. "Keep praying; I will join you, though for appearance's sake I need to remain outside." A brief smile flickered across her face before she returned to her post.

I turned my blurred vision back to The Beloved and continued to pray.

The second day was worse. Hunger gnawed at me, try as I might to turn every pang toward the ridding of the fire. And despite Sister Jenneth's unexpected compassion the previous night, the entire body of Sisters seemed content to never be seen by me. The bell around my neck jingled constantly as I walked, and once I heard a sudden scuffling of feet ahead of me, and when I turned the corner the hall was empty. As I looked, I heard a lock click in a door. I set my jaw, sent out a prayer, and continued on my way.

The list was endless: the guest dormitories, where travelers used to stay when our convent was a monastery, had been largely abandoned for years and the dust lay thick. In more than one room the window had been broken or left slightly open, and pigeon dung and feathers had crusted over everything. I found rats' nests, discarded bits of clothing and sandals, a broken whetstone, a broken human tooth, spots of dried blood, molded straw, desiccated bugs. The further I went, the dirtier it got, and the further away the well where I needed to refresh my bucket sometimes twice in one room. My feet grew hot, then tender, then sore. The skin of my palms and fingers tore. I had to force my back upright when I stood, and found myself sometimes walking with a hunch without realizing it. And above and around it all was a dread loneliness. I did not see another soul the entire day. And when I finally was able to go to my cell, utterly bedraggled, I found Sister Bethenny who was as stern, if not as harsh, as Sister Judith on the best of days. Now that she faced a long night's vigil over me, she appeared ready to bite through an uncooked artichoke.

"I did not see the fire today, Sister," I said quietly.

"You need not tell me what you don't see," she snapped. "Only tell me what you do. And nothing else," she added as I opened my mouth to reply.

I bowed my head, and went inside.

The following days grew worse and worse. There seemed to be a melancholy around the entire convent. The bell when it rang for

prayers barely seemed to send its echo over the walls, much less
through the entire valley. The winds were calm, and the birds and
bees stayed in their nests. The lambs on the hillside as I gazed out
one of the dormitory windows slowly followed their ewes, not one
frisky foot kicking up, and the rams huddled together listlessly. The
sky seemed dull, the sun bleak and distant. Great thunderclouds
were always on the horizon, though thankfully they did not yet come
near us.

Perhaps it was only me. I saw the world through eyes too accustomed to dirt and grime, to a holy convent seemingly bereft of souls.
I came here for the community it promised. But my curse came too,
and drove the community away. I wondered at my selfishness, that I
demanded to stay despite the effects I was having on the Sisterhood.

As I neared the end of the long hall at the topmost floor of the
dormitories, I found rooms that even the rats had left. Here was
only decay and filth, long abandoned. I had begun quartering the
rooms, spending one bucket on each corner before the long walk
back to the well. I could perhaps finish one room before two bells had
rung, but rarely. After Lentus, my foot missed a stair and I crashed
headlong to the bottom. As the bell at my neck stopped ringing, and
the throbbing in my head intensified, I knew I needed to simply
leave. Nothing was gained by staying. The fire still came to me at
odd times, whispering strange thoughts. Its actions were altered not
at all by my prayers and penances. And the silence of spending day
after day alone, except to be stared at as exhaustion pulled me into
sleep I didn't want, wore my spirit to a nubbin. And it would be three
more long days before we expected Mother Superior back from her
journey, to give my final sentence. I didn't think I could make it. I
didn't know why I wanted to.

By now, I knew the fire was there without it speaking, without me

seeing it. And it came to me then, in my broken heap at the bottom of
the stairs. It said nothing, but I felt my spirit harden. The throbbing
in my head eased, and the constant sting of broken skin on my hands
lessened. I took a deep breath as though on that first spring day when
we would throw open the windows and expel the stale winter air.
Another quick intake, and I got to my feet and retrieved my bucket.
There was only one more room to finish, and then I was to return to
the scullery.

As evening descended, and the bells of Scuros died away, I made
my way down the hall, already imagining the piles of cookware
awaiting me. My renewed determination had begun to fade. I still
wished desperately for companionship, and it still was nowhere to
be found. I had caught one fleeting glimpse of a black cloak disappearing around a door. I imagined the Sister's heart fluttering as she
fled so dangerous a creature as myself and nearly laughed, except I
cried.

All my imaginings paled when I pushed open the door. I wondered
what Sister Bethenny had even cooked with. It seemed to me there
were more dishes piled around the tables than had existed in our
convent. As I stared around in horror, I suddenly spied two beady
glistening eyes and a wiggling nose between two iron kettles. A head
peeped out, looking at me. Suddenly there was another, then a third.
They looked at me with greater curiosity and attention than any of
the Sisters had given me in nearly a week—with greater presence of
spirit than they had. I knew such dumb creatures did not possess
a soul, and yet I felt some strange companionship with them. Not
kindred, and yet it was as if they knew me somehow. Maybe because I
had been among their nests so much. I probably smelled like a rat—a
wet rat. Maybe because they were as despised and rejected as I was.

One set of eyes was replaced by a tail as the rat turned and walked slowly away. As if on cue, the second turned away, and the third. My spirit sank anew. I wished they would have stayed. Even the companionship of a rat was welcome to me, now.

Somehow, I didn't think that was the intent of the penance. I'm sure I was supposed to desire the companionship of the Sisters so much that I would return to them. But it was not up to me. And despite the comfort it had brought earlier, I cursed the fire now. In the dark scullery, my loneliness turned to bitter rage. And the fire never came.

Chapter 6

The next morning, I was carrying a slop bucket from the kitchens across the garden—it was slightly shorter than following the cloister. Though I felt I was stronger, my back still ached and so I struggled. The sun was just creeping over the walls, but most of the garden was still in a cold shade as I made my way to the main doors. There was a little brook outside the walls, to the south, where I was to dump the contents. My mind absent with thoughts of yesterday and tomorrow, I opened the door—and nearly dropped the bucket.

Thomas stood there, hand on the rope about to ring the small door-bell. He smiled when he first saw me; I saw his eyes drift, widening when he saw what was around my neck. "What do you wear that for?" he asked.

My eyes lowered in shame. "It's...I'm..."

"No, I'm sorry," he said. "My papa always says convent business is their own."

I dared a glance, saw chagrin in his eyes. Then they darted to the bucket in my hand.

"Let me help you," he said quickly, stepping forward and reaching out. My heart thrilled at first as his fingers met mind on the handle. Then it sank like a stone as I remembered the fire those fingers often held. He didn't know about me yet.

I drew back, and some of the contents sloshed onto my dress. He looked at me worriedly, a slight frown that pierced my heart creasing his usually-pleasant face in ways I hated to see. The frown softened into...shame? It looked like it, but it made no sense.

"I'm sorry," I said quietly. "You just surprised me." I tried to smile, worried it came off too false. I set the bucket down. "You can take it if you want."

He didn't smile, but he did take the bucket, and we walked toward the brook in silence. I wanted to tell him, hoping to find a friend. But even the rats abandoned me these days. We walked on and down into the short ravine to the stream.

He dumped the bucket, bent, and swirled some of the water in to rinse it out. He stood up again, and watched the waters go by for a time in silence. "I guess you heard," he said finally, quietly.

I cocked my head. I had thought to ask him the same thing, but he got there first. I knew some of the Sisters had already gone into town, and wondered if they had gossiped. But now he asked me? I wasn't sure I was ready for what he was about to say, and didn't want to prompt him. "I've not heard anything," I said honestly.

He turned on me swiftly, surprise and relief in his eyes. As he looked, though, the shame eventually crept back in, and his gaze dropped. "Oh," was all he said.

I fidgeted. "I thought, maybe, it was you who had heard. About me," I said. I felt myself trembling.

His gaze came up again, blank at first, then worried but curious.

"I've heard nothing," he said slowly.

"Oh. I wondered if the Sisters might have said something when they were in town a few days ago."

Again, worry with curiosity. And honesty. He shook his head. "I didn't know they had come. I mean, I never saw them. And I heard nothing from anyone I've spoken to. Are you okay? Are you leaving the convent?" There was strange hope in his last question. I couldn't entirely fault him; as long as I stayed, this, now, would be the extent of our friendship. But it nettled me too, that he seemed almost to wish me to make a choice that he wanted, and not—necessarily—what I wanted.

But the reality came back full-force. In that moment, I wished more than anything for him to take me in his arms and soothe me, to tell me everything would be all right. I didn't know if he would, or if he would recoil like everyone else. But he would have to know what was wrong before even having that chance. I had to make myself tell him.

I did, eventually. I met his eyes only occasionally. He had to pull more out of me than I intended. I wanted to be honest with him. But I was terrified. And then I saw him take a step backward, leaving the bucket between us.

"Please, Thomas," I said, my voice cracking. "Not you, too."

He scrubbed fingers through his hair. I met his eyes only briefly, seeing the frustration I should have expected. "You just told me you have fire living inside you," he said in a near whisper. "You want me to just say 'it'll be all right?'"

"Yes." I hated how pleading my voice sounded. I had only plead once before in my life.

There was silence except for the chuckling water. "It'll be all right," he said, quiet but sudden.

My eyes flashed to his. He was gazing at the stream, but I could tell he was watching me out of the corner of his eye. And he was serious. But it wasn't enough. I guess he knew it wouldn't be. And yet, it was something. A start.

"How?" I asked.

He drew a deep breath, and finally looked up and held my gaze. "I don't know," he said. "But it hasn't killed you yet, which is a good sign."

The corners of his lips quirked, and I laughed. And kept laughing, until I had to sit down. He sat down too, then moved the bucket aside. "I imagine the Sisters are trying to figure out how to rid you of it," he said, once our mirth subsided.

"Of course," I said sternly. "As I am."

"Why?"

Now it was my turn to stare. "Thomas! Seriously?"

He shrugged. "I just said it hasn't killed you. Hasn't killed or harmed anyone else."

"It's fire. Inside of me. That was burning on top of the gravestones of horrid evil men when I found it. What other reasons do I need? And if it hasn't killed me yet, maybe it needs me for a purpose." My eyes went wide. "Thomas, what if it needs me for a purpose?" The thought had never occurred to me, and it horrified me now. Another thought came, even worse, and I grew weaker. What if it waited, strengthened my resolve, only to keep me until Mother Superior arrived?

"What purpose could it have? How could you know or not know what purpose it might have?"

"Well, it talks...to...me..." I had forgotten to tell him—any-one—that, until now.

He didn't shift away this time. But he looked even harder at me.

"What does it say? Could you get it to talk to me?"

This was insane. "Thomas, why would you want to talk to it? And no, it's inside my head."

"Shame." He rubbed his palms on his trousers. "But it might help us figure out what's going on. With the thing that happened to you before, and the strange men in town."

"How would it know?"

"Do you think it doesn't?"

I almost wished he had just run away, rather than ask crazy questions. Except, he had a point, whether he knew it or not. "I guess it might, if it's tied up in all of it. That doesn't give me much hope that it doesn't have some dire and evil purpose in mind."

His gaze wandered a bit, and he chewed his lip. "I'm not—" He cut off, glancing quickly around and lowering his voice. "I think if it wanted to use someone for a dire purpose, it would have picked someone else."

"You're just saying that because you like me," popped out before I could stop it. I could feel the heat in my skin from my ears to the tip of my nose as I stared at the ground.

Through the throbbing blood in my ears I heard a faint rustle, and then his hand closed around mine. It was warm, a little calloused from hard work, but gentle. I pressed two fingers to my forehead. I needed some other focal point for my swirling emotions.

"I suppose you're right," he said quietly. "That because I like you, I want to help you, and try to ease some of your fears. Rae-Anna, despite anything I've been told or have learned about you and about the world, you're the kindest, purest person I've met. If evil wanted a minion, it couldn't have chosen a worse vessel."

I looked at him through a blur of tears. It was too much—too much kindness for who I was. I had done nothing except look pretty (so I was told) to warrant his bold claim. I wanted to believe it. I wanted it to be true. I wanted him. But it couldn't be. Not with fire inside me, and not with me inside a convent. "So you're saying you think it will be all right?" I smiled as I moved my hand out from under his, covering my retreat by wiping my eyes.

"You haven't told me what it says to you," he replied, mischief in his glance.

I sobered, wiped my eyes one more time, and took a breath. "It's strange," I said, as he sobered too. "I feel like it's words I recognize, but I can't think of where. It's usually only a phrase or two that it will say."

"Can you remember any of it?"

My mouth gaped one or two times. Now it came to it, I couldn't remember exact words. "Um, I guess not. Usually encouraging things. I felt like it gave me strength the other day when..." I trailed off, ashamed again—and still worried about why it sustained me. I didn't want him to know how hard the last few days had been. "When I didn't really want to keep doing what the Sisters were having me do. I was tired and a little bruised—"

"Which Sister?" he asked. I looked at him in surprise; his voice held more alarm than I thought necessary.

"It's not just one of them. They all agreed for me to do a sort of penance, I guess; cleansing. Trying to get the fire to leave. Why?"

He sat back a little. "Sorry. No reason. I won't hit any of them, if that's what you're worried about," he added with a laugh. I guess my worry showed through that clearly. "So it speaks words of strength and encouragement, in order that you will obey what the Sisters tell you to? Sounds evil, all right."

I opened my mouth to retort, then closed it. I wanted desperately to believe him.

"Well, hello," Thomas said quietly. I looked at him; he was looking at my hand. I instinctively buried it in my armpit. He, inexplicably, burst out laughing. I glared, then looked at my shoulder.

The fire had left my hand except for one tendril, and was perched on my shoulder like—I gulped—a rat. What was going on with the rats? Was the fire a rat-spirit of some kind?

It shifted, almost as if it turned to look at me and chide me. Rats wouldn't be as...knowing...as this fire seemed to be.

"Is it talking to you?" Thomas whispered.

I shook my head.

"Can I ask it a question?"

"Thomas, for Saint Petrif's sake—"

Forbid him not, to come unto me.

My eyes snapped to the fire. "Uh, I guess, apparently, you can," I breathed.

"Why are you here?" he asked.

I am come to send fire on the earth; and what will I, if it be already kindled? I repeated the words to Thomas, who clearly could not hear what was said.

"Why have you chosen Rae-Anna?"

There was silence for a moment, as if it were considering. I had never experienced it taking time to consider, before. I wasn't sure I wanted to know. Not to know positively. What if it answered that it was because I was cursed? Too many people said I was, and too much evidence proved it. If I was not cursed, too many questions would come flooding out. Too many phenomena would suddenly need a different explanation.

The silence from the fire continued. Thomas was looking at me expectantly. "Well? What did it say?"

"It hasn't said, yet," I replied. He must have noticed the hesitation in my tone.

"Does it usually answer more quickly?"

"If it doesn't just leave without answering." I couldn't help the bitter edge to my voice.

We sat in silence for a few more moments. "Can you tell us why you can't tell us?" Thomas asked suddenly.

I shook my head as the silence continued. I cocked my head, suddenly. It was so hard to tell with a mostly-formless fire, but it almost seemed like it was looking at me—as if waiting for me to do or say something.

"Rae-Anna," Thomas said suddenly, quietly. "You aren't cursed. It is not here for an evil purpose."

Something in his assuredness unlocked something inside me. I wanted to know. I needed to know. "Why did you choose me?" I asked. Pleading, again. I didn't like this new habit—

He that hath my commandments, and keepeth them, he it is that loveth me: and he that loveth me shall be loved of my Father, and I will love him, and will manifest myself to him.

I sat, too stunned to relay it to Thomas. It couldn't be. Not me. I was loved by no one—Thomas said I was pretty, like they all did. Maybe he cared about me. But no one cared enough to take personal interest in me unless I was doing something wrong. They certainly wouldn't care if I was doing some right—and I'm not saying I was. Besides, there was a convent full of women keeping his command-ments! That's all they did day or night.

The fire rose as if standing up, came closer, and—I don't know how else to say it—caressed my cheek. The thinking part of my brain said to recoil, but the heart of me leaned in. As tender as Thomas' hand had been on mine a moment ago, it felt a rough slap compared to the gentleness of this flame. The hope of love from his glances were daggers of hatred in this presence of infinity, a bottomless pool that invited me into such depths as I would never attain in this lifetime.

Instantly the presence was gone. I nearly fell over, catching myself barely before I toppled into Thomas.

"Rae-Anna!" shrilled across the field, and I shot to my feet as I recognized Sister Judith's voice. I fairly leapt sideways, away from Thomas, as he did the same. I could almost feel the ground tremble as she stormed toward us. Maybe it was my own trembling.

"How dare you insinuate yourself toward this boy," she seethed. "While still under our protection! You may not have made your vows yet, but we expect—"

"Sister, please," Thomas interrupted. A corner of me startled at the pleading tone dripping from the words.

"I will deal with you presently," she thundered. My eyes flicked sideways, having barely the time to register the shame on his face before her slap like a hundred stones put me on the ground with ringing ears.

"Go to your cell and wait until I come to you." Though I'm sure she shouted, it came to me only dully. When I looked up, Thomas was being hauled away. I think he argued for my honor. I do not think it mattered. As far as I knew, I had no honor, and never would.

Eventually I had the presence of mind to stand, and even to pick up the empty slop bucket before wandering back into the convent. Sister Judith would want me to go straight to my cell and lock myself in it, but then someone would need the bucket and not know where it was. I stopped beside the garden, over a field of brown and decay except for patches of chrysanthemums that bloomed in chill weather. I don't know why, but it came to me to desire to be such a flower—or like the twisted hornbeam, strong in the fiercest storms.

But my cheek still burned from the slap, my dress soiled from my collapse, my hands holding only a slop bucket, standing alone in front of a dying garden with an empty cell in a remote convent as my destination. My desires would have to learn to humble themselves.

I knew Sister Judith would be some time with Thomas—she always was—so I returned the bucket, then went to my cell. But I did not go inside, where I might accidentally lift my eyes to The Beloved. I could not bear the guilt that would assuredly come crashing from that height. The fire's caress and infinite presence was a lie. Probably a lie from the Dragon, now that I thought about it. His was a realm of fire. He had seduced the first with beautiful promises of significance and wisdom, and from those strength. And I was cursed. Thomas was wrong, and only said those things because of his lust for me. I emboldened him with my brazen temptations. I would lead him into darkness and death, and the fire only sought to bring us together to destroy us both.

I went instead to the railing of the cloister, looking again over the barren garden. The Sisters often talked about our role, here in the remote places, of fighting demons where they lived. It was in the Words, the demons wandering trackless wastes. I knew in the village some thought we went to escape—and, I suppose in truth, I had come here hoping to escape my curse. A fair lesson: we came here not to escape but to do battle. Except I was losing, and terribly. And my losing now threatened the rest of the convent, and Thomas, and perhaps the rest of the village. For who could know how far the demons would spread once they had victory?

A tear dripped onto my hand where I held onto the balustrade. There was perhaps another way to victory, also from the Words. I don't know why I recalled it, except perhaps it was the answer, given to me at the opportune time. Our Beloved had once banished a host of demons into a herd of pigs, and the herd rushed headlong to their deaths. And the man from whom the demons were banished was not again possessed. Could it not be that the demons died with the pigs? Could it not also be that the fire would die with me—and not the Sisters, or Thomas?

But would the demons take me with them? Pigs had no souls. And the Sisters certainly taught that suicides did not go to Our Father's realms—demon-possessed or not. Of course, the Sisters thought I was going to Abaddon anyway. At least Judith did. Why not rid the wilderness of Holden while I was at it? It seemed a noble thing to do, a righteous thing. Perhaps I would earn a place in The Trials instead. Perhaps Thomas could raise me to Heaven with his prayers. But he would have to know why I did what I did; otherwise he wouldn't bother praying, assuming I had gone to Hell as he would be taught.

My hands left the railing as I straightened. I had a purpose. For the first time since coming to the Sisters, I knew truly what I needed to do. But I had to hurry.

I turned and looked to the bell tower.

Chapter 7

I t is difficult to skulk with a bell around your neck. I knew this intuitively, yet I still tried. Silly, since only Judith knew I was supposed to be in my cell and she was occupied. I made my way toward the libraries for parchment and quill first. Then I would obey Sister Judith, if only long enough to leave the note.

It was uncomfortable, disobeying so much when I sought to be righteous. I worried it would all add up too much—that so much disobedience, and the suicide, would overrule whatever righteousness was attained by removing the demon presence from the convent. But it was the only choice I had.

It was also uncomfortable wearing that ridiculous bell in the normally-silent library. I briefly considered removing it. But that was one disobedience I could not stomach. All the Sisters, by agreement, commanded that penance. It would be disobedience to all, not just one. So I kept it on.

Only Sister Penelope, keeper of the books, was in the library when I entered. She glared at first, then seemed to remember why I had the bell. By then it was too late, so she sat stiffly while I went by, head down but glancing furtively. I went to the stacks where she kept useless parchments; this note was clearly not worth something shiny and new, and I would have needed a directive from another Sister to take one of those anyway. I took the top sheet, holding it up so she could see it (there were never many, and she liked to tabulate) then went to a writing desk.

I sat, thinking of what to compose. The difficulty would be whether they would read it to Thomas or not. If Sister Judith got to it first, she would read it and likely throw it away, especially if it contained some amorous contemplation.

My eyes fell to the page. It seemed someone had begun to copy from the Words, but had made some error and blotted it out. Not well, though, for I could make out the writing. I worried what it might say, and so I read:

"*Another parable put he forth unto them, saying, The kingdom of heaven is likened unto a man which sowed good seed in his field: But while men slept, his enemy came and sowed tares among the wheat, and went his way. But when the blade was sprung up, and brought forth fruit, then appeared the tares also. So the servants of the householder came and said unto him, Sir, didst not thou sow good seed in thy field? from whence then hath it tares? He said unto them, An enemy hath done this. The servants said unto him, Wilt thou then that we go and gather them up? But he said, Nay; lest while ye gather up the tares, ye root up also the wheat with them. Let both grow together until the harvest: and in the time of harvest I will sayeth...*"

There the writing stopped. I didn't know the Words well enough to know what error had been made. I had heard this story once, I believe, and didn't understand it then either. I knew little about gardening or sowing and reaping, but it seemed strange they could not pull the tares. I had certainly weeded many times, and once shown the weeds was never cautioned against accidentally uprooting the plants beside them.

I looked up to where Sister Penelope observed me from the corner of her eye. She didn't immediately look away, and she hadn't yet taken the opportunity to scuttle off to some dark corner, and that gave me hope. I continued to look at her until she turned toward me.

"Do you have a question?" she asked.

I smiled inside; I knew she would overlook my evil for the chance to dispense knowledge. "What is a tare?" I asked.

Her brow furrowed. "A rip?"

I looked at the page again, and shook my head. "It's spelled T-A-R-E."

"It's a kind of weed," she said.

"Why can't you pull it up without uprooting the wheat beside it?"

"Are you speaking of the parable?" she asked. I nodded. "Because our Beloved said it," she replied with finality, and turned away from me.

I chewed my lip. I was supposed to be preparing for my death. Uprooting the tares that had sprouted in our convent, and killing the wheat with it. *"Our Beloved said it."* He also said not to uproot them both, but to wait until the harvest. What harvest? Traditionally the harvest was the end of the age.

Sister Jenneth would know about wheat and tares. But I had no idea where she would be. Hers was the most itinerant of schedules, especially when growing season was past. But Sister Bethenny had grown up on a farm as well, I remembered. And she would be in the kitchen.

I stood and returned the parchment to the stack. "I ended up not writing on it," I said. She glanced at me critically. Worrying, probably, that I had descended into madness. "I might come back later for it," I offered lamely.

It was tempting to put a hand on my bell to silence it while I walked out, but thankfully I quickly realized what message that might send—if I did it then, might I do it some other time to creep up on a Sister unawares?

As I made my way toward the kitchens—taking the long way, I would not go through the Chapterhouse—another thought came to me: that the writing of the parable sounded of similar language and tone to the fire, when it spoke to me. That should have comforted me, perhaps, but I felt a chill. Was it possible that great evil could use the words of Our Father to lead me into darkness? The Liar had done so to the first children, I recalled, and had brought all the evil known into the world by one false step. What hope could I have, who had made innumerable false steps? What destruction was I bringing into this precious alcove, wittingly or not? I wavered, then, my footsteps ceasing as I looked again at the bell tower.

No, lest while you gather up the tares you also uproot the wheat with them.

I blinked away tears. It wasn't fair, to force us to grow up together. But the question came back with full force: why could they not be pulled separately? My steps resumed, still less-determined. I worried that Sister Bethenny wouldn't know, and I would have no more excuses.

As I turned to go through the door into the kitchens, I saw another swirl of cassock behind a door, another Sister hearing my bell and fleeing. It was becoming easier to ignore that. I admit I felt a twinge of guilt that Sister Bethenny would not be able to run, for she still had her duties.

"I only have a question," I called out when I thought I was in earshot. When I walked through the archway she was frozen in place, mid-stir. "I'm sorry, Sister, but I only have a question that I hoped you could answer, since you grew up on a farm."

She harrumphed, but continued stirring. It smelled delicious, and I knew I wouldn't get any. But that wasn't why I was here. "Why can't you pull up tares without uprooting wheat? And why would you let them both grow until the harvest? Won't they choke out the wheat?"

Her stirring faltered as she eyed me. When she continued I thought she might ignore me as the silence stretched. "Tares, when they are small, look just like wheat," she said. "It's not that they uproot each other, but that the harvesters wouldn't be able to tell the difference. Only once they've matured are they distinguishable. And yes, a field with tares produces less crop, but not as little as a field that has had most of the crop pulled out."

"Then how did they know there were tares if they look the same?"

She paused again, this time clearly considering. "Well, it is still a parable," she mused. "But a good farmer will also know when a crop is sprouting thicker than what they've sown. But mostly I think it was a parable. One, obviously, still with great truth." She eyeballed me again. I'm not sure why she thought I would be impertinent. Although, it had been some time since I had shown genuine interest in the Words of Our Father.

So. Perhaps The Beloved was cautioning me against suicide because, what? I still had a crop to produce? That the demons inside me would have to be allowed to grow until I could distinguish what was wheat sowed by Him and what was tares sown by The Liar? It seemed too simple. And it didn't rid me of the fire, or reconcile me to the Sisters.

"If you're going to just stand there, you may as well start cleaning up," Sister Bethenny said.

I startled. "Sister Judith ordered me to my cell," I admitted. "I was going there next, but I had to put back the slop bucket, and—"

She waved me off quickly. "I'll answer to her if she comes looking. I need pots scrubbed. Get to it."

"Thank you, Sister," I said honestly. Scrubbing pots alone was still better than sitting in my cot alone.

I hurried down the short flight of stairs into the cellar. Distracted as I was with fetching water and soap and the brush—we needed a new one soon, there was more board than bristle by this point—I was only barely aware of soft squeaks and the scuttling of tiny feet. But soon it arrested my attention as more and more made their way into the room. I paused and looked, then froze: near the wall was a low shelf for cookware, now empty except for a line of rats, more than a dozen, all staring blankly at me as their paws scratched the wood rhythmically, mechanically. In unison. Like the drumbeats from my vision of druids when this horrid nightmare first began. But they seemed to me mere puppets, their limbs shackled too, like the dancers, but not shackled to me. As I watched they grew more frenzied, their whiskers vibrating, and I could tell they were held against their will.

Suddenly they began moving separately, their paws no longer scratching in straight lines. I began to realize they were not just pawing the wood, but making marks in it. A few, as their claws were strained too far, began pawing with bloody toes and the blood mixed in with the wood. I could only watch in growing horror as their scratches took shape. They were writing, each rat a letter, so I came to know there were seventeen. My heart at first beat faster, then slower as I wished I had simply jumped off the tower and taken the demons and the mystery of the tares with me.

Finally they stopped and stepped back from their awful work. There, on the shelf, with tattered wood and blood they had written:

"ALL HAIL LORD OF FIRE."

When I raised my hand in terror, it was wreathed in terrible flame. I heard a shriek behind me and turned so startled I barely recognized Sister Judith before, in reflex, I reached out and grabbed her arm. Her shriek cut off almost unnaturally as we gaped at each other.

"I thought you were The Dragon come to..." I snatched my hand back, the one covered in fire. But she continued to gape, and the veins of her neck throbbed. "I'm sorry, Sister," I said, feeling a sob stick hard in my throat. I looked up, and she continued to gape, her veins continued to throb, her face now grew crimson, and she began to vibrate.

I took another step back as she choked and sputtered, then finally began to scream. Fire sprayed from her wrists, from her elbows—from every joint of her limbs. Not like my blue flame but like the sparks from striking flint, multiplied by thousands. They grew to white-hot flames, and blinding light shot from her mouth and eyes as though the fire were inside her head and couldn't get out.

My own screams blended with hers, and I ran. Up the stairs and through the kitchen, feet scrabbling, I eventually managed to shape my screams into cries for help. Sister Bethenny was gone. The garden and cloister were empty. But the walls echoed with my voice, now ragged, and soon filled also with the sounds of running feet.

Sister Lucy was the first to come upon me, and I collapsed sobbing into her arms. I couldn't answer her if I wanted to, and part of me did not want to. What could I say? My only defense against this fire had been that it had harmed no one. But finally, when she shook me and demanded I let her go and tell her what happened, I could only point toward the kitchen.

"Fool girl," she said. "Take us there." For by now a clutch of Sisters had come, standing awkwardly distant but obviously curious.

I shook worse than the last leaf of autumn, but made myself go forward. When I entered the kitchen Sister Bethenny had returned, and I could tell from her look that she had gone to see.

"Sister Lucy," she said weakly, then shook her head.

"What is it?"

She shook her head again, then took an interrupted breath. "Don't take them all down there," she said, glancing at the rest of the Sisters. Her eyes then turned hard on me. "Just that one. And be vigilant."

I glanced back, and Sister Lucy's lips pressed into a hard line. "Very well. Lead on, girl."

I truly didn't want to. I didn't want to see the charred body. I had seen meat burned in a fire before, and I didn't want to see Sister Judith—harsh as she was—in such a state.

I needn't have worried.

When Sister Lucy finally shoved me down the steps—not harshly, but firmly—all that remained was a pile of black ash in the shape of a body. The writing was still on the shelf, though, and Sister Lucy saw it almost instantly.

"Who is this?" she demanded.

"Sister Judith," I said miserably.

Sister Lucy's gaze on me suddenly...softened? Did I paint so abject an image?

"Did you write that? No, your fingers aren't bloody. Tell me, if you can, what happened."

Somehow, I managed. Bewildered, not just from the incident itself but from Sister Lucy's reactions. She should be terrified. Repulsed. Something. Not simply curious. What could it mean? I wanted to die even more than ever, and she seemed almost ready to take the bell off and reinstate me. I couldn't fathom it.

"I'm cursed, Sister, and I brought it here and now it's only grown worse. Please let me leave or let me die or..." I trailed off into tears.

"Well, we cannot do that just yet," she muttered, "though this is a fine mess." She sighed. I imagined she was trying to think up a suitable punishment—to what end, I didn't know. I had killed a Sister, and not pleasantly. At least, not quickly. "Go to your cell for now. I need to see to cleaning this away, and then I'll come see you. Keep yourself alive until then, yes?" she asked wryly.

I couldn't understand it, but still shocked by the whole event I nodded and trudged away. A few of the braver Sisters had by now come partway down the stairs.

"And take off your bell, please," Sister Lucy called after me.

I turned to see her looking at me expectantly. But my hands wouldn't move. I couldn't make my fingers work the cord. Sister Lucy tsked and nodded her head to Sister Jenneth. She approached with far greater confidence than she'd had when the fire first appeared—certainly far greater confidence than I had now—and quickly undid the knot. She unceremoniously chucked the bell across the floor and it seemed to me to clang with great clappers as it bounced into a far corner. I stared at her and she sniffed.

"Incessant thing," she said. I saw no compassion or forgiveness in her eyes, and yet her features shared a similar softness to Sister Lucy's. But before I could think to ask, she jerked her head toward the kitchens and turned resolutely to Sister Lucy.

I wasn't sure if thanks were in order, so I left and went to my cell to await the next inexplicable event.

Chapter 8

I didn't have long to wait. Sister Olivia came first to check if I had wounds. I had to undress and turn slowly for her inspection.

"What are these?" she snapped suddenly. I looked awkwardly at my elbows.

"Oh. One day while cleaning the guest dormitories, I slipped coming down the stairs."

She glared at me. "And you didn't seek healing?"

"I didn't know they were that bad," I admitted. "I didn't feel they were that bad, and I didn't look. And...I didn't want to get too near to any of you."

Her jaw tightened. "Of course. The rest of these look as old; are they from the same incident?"

I looked quickly at where she pointed with a short rod, and nodded.

"Get dressed. And tell me about your hands; Sister Lucy says there were words scraped into wood, down below, but you didn't do it. Your hands seem to tell a different story, though."

I pulled the shift over my head and glanced quickly at my fingers. They were rough, but just from normal work. "I've been busy, Sister," I said. Now that I had contemplated death, and saw little place for myself in this world, I found I cared less to defer to the Sisters. I picked up my dress and donned it as I continued. "I've scrubbed every corner of the dormitories, cleaned stick litter from the gardens, washed uncountable pots, pans, plates, and bowls. How should my hands look?"

She glared at first, and I didn't blame her. But then she simply relaxed. "Let me see them." She held out a hand. I reached out, then drew back reflexively.

"The last Sister I touched burned to ash," I said.

"Yes. Well. Never mind. I mean, just hold them so I can see them; I won't touch them."

I looked at her curiously as she inspected my trembling fingers. She hummed once or twice as she looked. "Sister," I said hesitantly. Her eyes barely flicked up. "Why are you doing this? I mean, why was I not...I don't know..."

"Punished?"

"Killed."

She nearly rolled her eyes. "We're far from that. For one thing, we cannot kill each other without Mother Superior's consent. At least, we're not supposed to."

That silenced me, briefly at least. But I had to go on. "But, it's almost as if you aren't surprised at Sister Judith's death—or, aren't—"

She cut me off with a sharp wave. A dark storm rose in her eyes. "Do you say we wished her dead?"

I did. The admission horrified me. I had, at times, wished her dead. At first I only wished she would leave the convent; when that became an impossibility... "I don't think I mean that," I said weakly. "But—"

"I can tell you were not wounded in this event, and did not scratch the letters yourself, even if you had done so in an unconscious possession," she said harshly. "I will inform the Sisters of my findings." She rose and left, fairly slamming the door behind her.

I sat in stunned silence for a while. And yet, there was *something* wrong. They had treated me far worse just for having the fire to begin with; now that it had killed someone, they seemed to accept it. Why? I wanted it gone far more than ever, wanted myself gone far more than ever. Any doubt that this thing was demonic was erased. The rats hailed it, the rats that had kept those evil dead men company in the catacombs—had kept them company and yet fled from me at first. Only after the fire did they seem to find interest in me. Now they saw me as their lord? My curse was far worse, went far deeper, reached far further than my worst terrors. And instead of being rid of me, they removed the cursed bell, ensured I wasn't harmed—

The door opened, and Sister Bethenny entered with a steaming tray. And they fed me? She set the tray down, then sat down wordlessly. When I only looked at her, she pointed her gaze to the tray.

I couldn't understand it. If anything, I desired food even less than life. But I thought she wouldn't leave until the tray was empty; she certainly seemed firmly planted. So I picked up a slice of bread and bit.

I didn't know what she had done with it, but I ate so ravenously that I only remember the first bite, and then it was gone. I vaguely remember notes of honey and toasted almond. They had never been so extravagant with me—to my knowledge, they had never been so extravagant with anyone. I took the cup and drank deeply; it tasted like a pale wine, almost sweet and fruity. I was careful not to gulp, and yet it called to my senses like the purest cold water I had ever tasted.

I looked up. Sister Bethenny sat erect, her eyebrows climbed nearly to her wimple. "I'm sorry, Sister," I said. It took everything in me
not to wipe my mouth like a glutton. I set the cup down gently. "I
guess I was...I haven't eaten in some time."

"Forty days and forty nights, I would say," she replied with a wry
twist to her mouth. "Are you tired? Are your thoughts confused?"

"I feel refreshed," I said. "And my confusion is understandable, I
think." My bullishness had returned.

Sister Bethenny settled back again. "Yes, a strange thing, under
normal circumstances. It has perhaps been a long time in coming,
though."

"I was afraid of this since I first saw it," I agreed. "Seeing where it
was, upon whom it rested...I was surprised that it didn't kill me."

Sister Bethenny blinked, and I realized she hadn't been looking at
me. "Oh, the fire? Yes, we were all worried it might do something like
this, of course. It seems strange how we've all come to...not accept it,
but... Well, daughter, it has become a part of you, hasn't it?"

I looked down at my hands. She was right. Terrifying though it
was, much as I wanted it gone, believed it was demonic, it almost
seemed inappropriate that the blue fire wasn't there. So. Cursed by
Our Father, friend to rats and fallen Brothers also cursed—

I looked up sharply. "You called me...daughter?"

She seemed as surprised as I was. "I did. It..." She trailed off,
looking at me in a kind of abject wonder.

"Sister, this is making less sense than what the fire did to Sister
Judith. I am cursed! Demon-possessed, it seems like. And yet you see
me as nearing Sisterhood? This is not the convent I thought it was
when I came here—"

"Let me stop you before you say something we all regret," she
said. Her eyes were alight now, her back straight. I sat back, wilted.

She took a deep breath. "Your words are truer than you know, but not in the way you think. In truth, child, we don't know what to do with you. You have done all we asked, and as near as we can tell without the slightest fault. Sister Aitrinn even caught you doing above and beyond our decrees. By all our ken you display all the fruits of righteousness and peace. And this thing with Sister Judith—" She cut off, her lips compressing. "Well, there is far more to the story than you know—or can know, at least yet. We are afraid of the fire, to be sure, and so we isolate you. The risk to us all, directly on the heels of such a display of power and intuition..." Her lip trembled. She sniffed, and it firmed. "We're doing the best we can. We will tend to you for now, until we decide what is best for ourselves, and for the convent. Give me your tray."

Too stunned to speak, I held it out. Her fear, I noted, felt far more personal than mine—that she might be the next one to burn. But surely such a holy person would be safe from a demonic flame? But then, they all should have been. Why Judith? Did her faith waver in that moment, give opportunity for the fire to devour her? Surely Our Father had not chosen to abandon her—He was always faithful. Did she attribute too much power to me? To the rats? By having more "faith" in their power, perhaps her faith in the power of The Beloved and Father waned and was overcome. Were the other Sisters, then, afraid of such a lapse in faith, and their own subsequent vulnerability? It made sense. But why would she then consider me a daughter automatically? As if she felt a near-kindred spirit in me?

Another knock. This time it was Sister Penelope, and she came in with an armful of books. She glanced around the room and huffed, ignoring me for several moments as she searched. Finally she looked at me petulantly. "Can I use your pillow?"

I gaped a moment. "Um, of course," I said, waving a hand at it.

She stood another moment. "Put it on the floor. Beside the chair. Please."

I obeyed, and she gently set the books atop it before settling herself in the chair. She picked up the first tome and thumbed through it. "Um. Here. Do you...no, that's the wrong one. This: do you, Rae-Anna, affirm and attest you will speak to me—to the Sisters of this Convent—truly and without duplicity; that you will seek the advancement of the Gospel of Our Beloved and Our Father; that you will act toward all those, inside and outside, with charity and goodwill; that you will forsake all earthly ties in pursuit of the heavenly; and in so denying yourself seek to become one with The Beloved and wedded to him alone?"

She looked up. My jaw had been dropping lower and lower as she read, and snapped shut now. They were the vows of Sisterhood. But I was to have another few months before pronouncing those. *And I had just killed a Sister!* Why did it seem that no one grasped this? Why was I still here? Why was I not in chains?

She waited my answer. But I had not yet decided. *Forsake all earthly ties...including Thomas.* That was what I had not yet decided. I knew I didn't love him, I was attracted to him. And yet there was a sense, however girlish it might be, that I was meant to love him at some future time. I know that sounds coldly logical, and it was. And yet...

"Rae-Anna," Sister Penelope called, and I sensed a warning in her tone. "Are you unable to make these vows?"

So that was it. By rejecting the vows it could seem as though I hesitated for evil reasons. If I accepted them gladly, it meant The Beloved was at work in me. "Sister," I said. "I know what my hesitance looks like. But anyone else is given the full year, even without circumstances like mine. How can I commit to a convent, to a Sisterhood, when I might possess within me their destruction?"

"And what if the vows would take the fire from you? Perhaps it lingers because you waver."

"But those vows go far deeper than that. Of course, if we knew it would rid me of this fire, I would take them; but I had not been ready to vow before the fire came, and those hurdles remain even with that gone."

She snapped the book shut. "Very well. It was worth a try, I thought." She set the book down and picked up the next. "Let's try to understand this fire better, then. I thought we acted rashly before, but Sister...well, haste seemed wise. To some." Her mouth hung open, then shut as she looked down and paged through the book. "Did you know the northerners had many different words for fire?" she said absently as she continued to look. "The fire of the hearth is different from the forest fire is different from a campfire on a cold winter night. They each have a very different purpose." She fixed me in a hard stare for a moment. "And we must not confuse a fire sent to destroy with a fire sent to comfort." She returned to her book. "But all fire can be sparked, if one has the proper tools. So listen carefully, and try to feel each word." She began to read, and the language she spoke first reminded me of the language I'd heard in the catacombs, and a terror filled me to hear those strange voices again. I almost cried out to her to stop, but as the words came to my tongue I felt a sudden sense of holy disdain. This fire was not so easily conjured—was not conjured in the slightest, but moved according to its divine and highest will.

I let her finish as I tried to damp a sense of pride I knew was inappropriate and uncharitable. And there was no fire. When she looked up I only allowed a mildly compassionate grin, almost apologetic, to curve my lips. "I don't think this fire is ours to order around," I said quietly. "It has always come and gone at will—its own will."

She took another deep breath, and snapped shut that book as well. "Fine," she said, bordering on anger now. "Can you ask it, if it so deems, to grace us with its presence—" She cut off with a small yelp as blue flame raged on my hand.

I held it away from both of us; I didn't want to harm her, and I was afraid it would harm me. I think I even convinced myself it was burning my hand. But no; it limned my hand but did not actually touch the skin. Even now there was a war in my mind, knowing I should be repulsed by this thing, terrified of it, terrified of what it meant that I had it. But I struggled to actually do so.

"Why did you want it to come?" I asked with far greater calm than I thought I should have.

She stared a moment and took a deep breath. "We had hoped to...test it," she said. "To see the limits of...well, how easily it could hurt us. It doesn't burn?" I shook my head. "I see. Can you set anything on fire with it? Try the candle."

Again it seemed to look at me, as though there—but there was! There was a face in the fire, this time. Not a human face, but vaguely traced by the flames I thought I could see something of eyes. And yet, not human eyes, just the awareness, the knowledge that there was an aspect to this fire, a presence. A sentient, will-bearing presence. I felt suddenly foolish, the same as if Sister Penelope asked me to push another Sister's face into a bowl of water to see if she would drink. But as soon as I felt that, I also felt an encouragement. For some reason this fire was suddenly ready to demonstrate a few things. So I took a deep breath and held it out.

As soon as the edge of the fire touched the wick, sparks flew again as it had with Sister Judith. I yanked my hand back in fear as Sister Penelope yelped. But the sparks died instantly into the plainest orange flame, and burned like any other candle.

Sister Penelope rose, and I shifted my hand to keep it well away from her. She held a hand over the candle. "Hmm. Heat. But your fire puts none out. Let's see..." She picked up another candle and lit it from the one I had lit, and muttered: "it acts like any other fire." She took a step back and considered my fire. "See if it will burn your linens," she said.

My mouth worked a few times. But I saw the determination in her jaw, and also felt a reassurance from the flame. Come to think of it, it hadn't burned my blankets before when I buried it among them. I brought it down hesitantly. It shifted around my hand, retreating from the bedding. I began to pull a cover over it, and it winked out. Surprised, I pulled the blanket away. It returned almost immediately, seeming to seep out of my skin before hovering over it again.

"It didn't do that before," I said, looking into its visage curiously. "Another time, I had my hand completely under the blanket and it just burned underneath."

Sister Penelope hummed as she returned to her seat. "So perhaps it has grown in either power or presence," she mused. I looked a question at her. "Well," she continued, "it could touch things before without burning them; now it seems to burn anything it touches. As if it were unable to interact with things beforehand but can now. The question, obviously, is why."

"And how?" I asked.

"This thing is clearly not of this world—not our waking world," she said, picking up another book. "Whether from heaven or hell, or some other place, it has entered here with only limited ability at first. It could speak to you? But only in your mind." I nodded. "I wouldn't be surprised if it could do more, soon, speaking audibly or impressing its will on others around you. What sort of things has it said to you?"

"Comforting things," I said quickly. "Giving me peace or strength as I needed. It also...promised things..."

She snapped the book shut. "What sort of things?"

"Um, that I would live...and...that against those who afflict the widows or fatherless his wrath will wax hot."

She merely raised an eyebrow. "Well that promise seems fulfilled, doesn't it?"

I nodded vaguely. "I didn't think Sister Judith oppressed..." But I couldn't say it. She had; I denied it for so long because she was a Sister.

"I'm glad to hear you say that," Sister Penelope replied. "Can you burn anything that you aren't touching? Can you throw the fire?"

I blinked at her rapid transition. Again, the Sisters seemed loath to discuss Sister Judith at length. And, again, I felt foolish for what she was asking me to attempt. I waved my arm, though, in some sort of throwing motion. The fire stayed with me, did not even flutter as a normal flame would.

"Concentrate," she urged. "Try to convince the fire to light something distant from you."

I stared at her, and I confess the fire did as well. I cannot think the image we presented, both of us casting withering glances at Sister Penelope, but it was effective. She actually bowed her head.

"I'm sorry," she said; I didn't know if she meant it for me or the fire. I remained silent. And, suddenly, she looked up as though forgiven. After a pause, the fire departed. She took a deep breath. "Well, that is strange indeed," she said. She looked at me with a new light in her eyes. "As I suspected: its power grows in this world. No wonder you haven't been rid of it yet. I will make my report."

She gathered up her books and left without another word or glance. I stared at my hands. This time I did not startle at the knock on my door.

Sister Lucy walked in without waiting for response; it was her right. With Sister Judith gone, she would oversee the convent until Mother Superior's return. "A strange day," she said.

"A few of them," I said. When she barked a laugh, I looked up.

"I do apologize, daughter," she said, very intentionally. "We've never heard of the things that have been happening of late. We're not sure how to respond."

"I know."

She nodded once. "I suppose you do. But from what the other Sisters have told me, you are not harmed, and you will not willingly harm. What happened—"

"I killed a Sister," I said, glaring. "And everyone goes about as if nothing has happened! Well, not nothing," I admitted. "But only as if I raised my voice to her or acted impudently, or disobeyed her word. And as one you refuse to explain why."

Sister Lucy clasped her hands tightly. "You are still a daughter only," she said. "It comes difficultly for us to try to explain ourselves to you—that we ever needed to. You would have learned in your own time, perhaps. And until Mother Superior returns I will continue to let you learn in your own time. Do you think you should learn everything immediately?"

"It would be nice," I muttered.

She looked critically at me. "Would it? Would it be nice to be granted all knowledge all at once—when you have not the wisdom to apply the knowledge you have? I praise Our Father that He only reveals to us what we can handle—with His grace, of course. What He does we do not always know, but later on we will know what He is doing."

I glanced up sharply; the fire had said a similar thing to me, but in its strange cadence. But before I could ask, she held up a necklace. "Do you recognize this?" she asked.

I peered at it, a fine silver chain with a simple blue gem dangling at the end. I shook my head.

She withdrew it. "It seems to be the only part of Sister Judith that survived. Not even blackened by soot. We wondered if you had dropped it." She gazed at me another moment longer. "Until we know Mother Superior's will, we still are hesitant to administer no penance for what happened today. We must seem to be doing our best. So for the next few days you will work as scullery-maid." She turned to leave, and paused. "And please be careful what you touch, will you?"

Chapter 9

I woke early. The morning was still dark and cold, and yet I felt rested and...cleansed. Not just me, and not even just my cot and blanket. After dressing and exiting my cell the air itself felt lighter and purer. But even as I enjoyed this sense, another snuck in; there was some lingering heaviness. A cloying, only noticeable if you held the scent in your nose and let it fester.

But the heaviness was not upon me yet, and so I went to the kitchens. Sister Bethenny had not yet arrived, so I lit a few rush lights and made my way into the scullery. I glanced at the blackened spot on the floor a little distantly; for some reason I had been allowed to remain, and she had not. It frightened me that I took it so calmly, now. And yet, the logic was there. I truly had not meant to harm her, had reached out purely in reflex.

I looked and saw the words still scratched in the shelf. I wondered that it hadn't been scoured yet. None of us were true carpenters, but we could do our part. I certainly didn't want any man from the village to come and see the words. And I was considered a daughter, now;

expected to act like a Sister though I had not taken vows.

I went back up and out to our little workshed, and retrieved a rasp. The rats' claws were not strong and had not cut too deep: seven or eight passes apiece obscured the letters enough. Time, and placing and replacing pots and pans, would do the rest. Then I took a brush and our harshest lye and scrubbed the soot from the floor.

I heard Sister Bethenny arrive above, but kept working. I believe she looked in on me—there was the briefest passing of shadows in the dim light—but she said nothing and I soon heard the clanking and clattering of pans and ladles as she began to prepare breakfast.

A sluice of clean water washed the foam away. The soot now clung only to small cracks and crevices. Cleansed. The word kept floating across my mind, and I wondered at it.

I climbed the stairs to the kitchen. Sister Bethenny didn't look up. "Are you satisfied?" she asked. I stared, surprised and wounded at the question. I thought they...?

She looked up, then rolled her eyes. "Is it clean down there now? Halls of Heaven, girl, no one blames you for what happened."

"Why not?" I asked. It was habit, now; I didn't expect an answer. And, as I began to help with the task, I didn't receive one.

Sister Bethenny punched the dough a few times, then sighed. "In truth, we blame ourselves." She shook her head and continued kneading. "We are bound, sometimes. Bound not to talk to outsiders. Until you make your vows, you are an outsider. And yet..." She flipped the dough, punched it again. "Yet you're bound up in it tighter than anyone. There was much talk—had been, months ago—of expelling Sister Judith."

I set a pitcher of water down hard, sloshing it and nearly knocking over our small supply of sugar. "Why?"

But I was met again with tight-lipped silence. I finally found motion again, and busied myself preparing a thin gruel. My mind couldn't help returning to the men in the crypts. Surely she had not done such terrible things as those? She was just harsh, perhaps hindering me too much for what Our Father might have called me to—risking my conversion. But she had certainly not been the only one. Other Sisters were just as harsh in silence as she had been in voice. Why none of them? Or had it simply been none of them, yet? They would fear me for that.

"I've said more than I should already," Sister Bethenny said finally, quietly. "It should only be another day or two, and you will have all the answers we can be allowed to give you. Lighten your conscience for now with this, though: it had been within the power of others to prevent last night's occurrence, and they did not. And stop putting so much water in the pot; the meal should still have some substance to it." She offered a small, chiding grin. Though I did not return it—I was only a daughter, not a Sister—I found renewed focus on my work, and busied myself the rest of the morning.

Gemmans and Quard bells passed. The sun was high, but still cool and distant. Snows would be upon us before long, and much would need to be done to caulk us against bitter winds. As I hurried along the cloister, worrying at the naked branches of our little garden trees, the gate bell rang.

Our door had never been so busy. That worried me somewhat too. Changes, all coming together, unsettled the routine and there was no telling where it might land. And what if this visitor had some shadowed past as well? Might I burn them alive?

I shook my head. This was becoming too-comfortable a line of thought. I peered through the grate, and my heart leapt: Thomas, come again. Only this time, we could not be interrupted by...

Shameful thought! Too comfortable. I opened the door. "Good

morning, Thomas," I said as demurely as I could. I was expected to act as a Sister would. "What brings you today?"

"Some news," he said. Difficult news, by his tone. Little did he know.

"Let me take you to Sister Lucy, then," I replied. She would be the one to hear such things now. He straightened, a curious look in his eye. He wondered, I could tell, yet he also showed relief. I didn't blame him. I gave a reassuring smile. "I'll let her explain it to you," I said. "Please follow."

I went ahead, bringing him to Sister Lucy's study and announcing him. I departed; I would need to be in the kitchens soon to help prepare the noon meal. I tried to put him out of my mind, and yet I wondered what news he brought. The village seemed as busy with events as we were—events that might involve us, strangely enough. It must concern the strange men who had come along looking for the bodies of the men below.

And why would they want them? Surely one would not pay any sort of respect to them, or want anything they had been buried with, or want to leave anything. Perhaps part of a genealogy?

I couldn't worry about that, too; I had too much else on my mind. Sister Lucy would tell me, or not. Or maybe Thomas would. My heart leapt at that thought as it had when I saw him at the door.

I hurried on, head bowed. I had too much else on my mind. I couldn't think of that either.

I went to my cell for contemplation and prayer, and to wait for noon meal preparation. I worried my mind would be too busy. But I gazed on The Beloved and all thoughts and worries departed. His single-minded focus on his Father's kingdom radiated from that singular image of sacrifice, a focus I often envied. How much could I accomplish if I could only dedicate myself? Visions flashed through my head, bestowed upon me by the Sisters of the convent and the lives they led. And yet none of them stuck, none of them appealed. None of them called. Bit by bit, the flickering blue flames came to mind, asserting by degrees their importance. I had certainly done everything I could to rid myself of them. They seemed destined to stay. But even as that thought came to me, it changed, seemed true and yet false. A permanent impermanence.

I felt a little dizzy at the sensations. A shadow fell across me; I had left the door open to help me gauge when it was time to leave. My meditations had apparently been too focused. "I'm coming, Sister; I'm sorry I'm late."

But when I turned, it was Thomas who stood cautiously in the doorway. "Sister Lucy sent me to you," he said. "She said I should talk to you."

"Did she?" I asked, still a little dizzy. I stood carefully, folded my hands. I was about to invite him in, but I knew that wouldn't do. Instead I gestured toward the garden. He shuffled with an embarrassed grin, and let me proceed. My heart fluttered as I passed him, and I cast him a nervous smile. "Sorry, excuse me," I said.

I shook my head at myself: supposed to act like a Sister, indeed. Still a child, despite what had happened. I straightened, tried to shake off my girlish fantasies. Single-minded focus. The image of The Beloved came to mind, and I sobered. We found a bench, and sat.

"Did she say what we were to talk about?" I asked.

He could sense the change in me, and matched it. He never did push, much as it seemed he admired me. He was the first in my life to do that.

"She said there was some strange news around her elevation to position," he said. "Something happened to Sister Judith?"

Did I imagine a hard edge to his voice when he said the name? It seemed like I didn't, but her name never rang lightly against my ears. "She told you nothing?" I asked, genuinely surprised. But I remembered: she wouldn't know I had told Thomas about the fire. When he shook his head, I continued, telling him the events from the time she took him away from me yesterday until this morning.

I waited for another pull-back from him, a new fear. But instead he gazed across the garden and drew a deep, relieved sigh. Though he looked aside I could see a new light in his eyes, one I thought I saw usually hooded. Now and again it would flare up when he looked at me, but would damp down again. Now it blazed forth bright and clear, and his shoulders squared.

"Well," he said, but as though he spoke to himself. "That's done."

"Thomas?" I asked. He was acting like the Sisters had, except free from the guilt they displayed. When he turned his eyes on me, and the light from his eyes struck me, I had to look aside myself. Single-minded focus. "Why does everyone seem happy she is dead? Or at least relieved," I amended quickly.

"They—no one told you?" he asked.

So he knew, too? "They said I was an outsider, still, not allowed into all the secrets they kept. Just that..." I didn't know if I should tell him what Sister Bethenny told me. They would view him as even more outside. I shook my head. "No one has told me much, just that she was not the Sister I thought she was."

He hesitated. "What kind of Sister did you think she was?" he asked.

"She was harsh," I admitted freely. "She treated me I felt unfairly, but I was only a child. I don't know." I hadn't let myself think about her much, for there were usually only bad thoughts, thoughts I assumed were because of her great height and my great depth.

"Did you respect her? Look up to her?" He pressed now, though his voice was still gentle.

"She was a Sister," I said, frustrated in full now. "I was told I must; that if I didn't it was because of my sin."

"Told that by who?"

I stared at him. The light in his eyes was intense, now, commanded my honesty. I felt my back stiffen as my chin came resolutely up. "By Sister Judith," I said. We held each other's gaze for a moment before bursting into laughter.

"An unbiased opinion if ever I heard one," Thomas said finally. Now that I said it out loud, it was ludicrous. I couldn't believe I hadn't seen it before. "Well," he continued as our chuckles subsided. "You may be an outsider to them; so if you are, then you are one with me." His cheeks colored a moment before he continued. "We are both outsiders, and can speak freely to one another." He sobered completely, now, and drew a deep breath. For a long moment I thought maybe he had reconsidered; his hooded gaze bent unseeing on the dead trees of the garden. "It doesn't make it easier," he said finally. I almost didn't hear him. "You've told me of your fire," he said, his voice a little stronger. "That took vulnerability, and trust. Allow me, please, to be vulnerable with you, and trust you."

I wanted desperately to take his hand, to hold him close—not for my sake, but for his. Every fiber of me pushed toward him, but I made myself sit still. I could not stop the words from coming out of my mouth, though. "I will love you no matter what," I heard myself say.

For a wonder—and a pity—the earth did not open up and swallow me. Thomas, for a wonder and a pity, did not take my hand or take me into his arms—or confess the same. And yet, by mere fact that he did not take advantage of a slip of my tongue, he told me more than words that he felt the same.

Instead, he studied me a moment, then grinned impishly. "As a Sister, right?" he asked.

"Of course," I stammered, unable to match his grin. But I could tell he understood.

"Sister Judith was far worse than only harsh," he said. Again, the hesitation, the sobering. She must have done something terrible to him—but what could it have been? "You know she spent a lot of time with me," he began slowly.

"She was always interested in news from the village," I said, uncertain where he was going.

He grunted. "Right. Always news that I had to give in the privacy of her chambers, away from you or any of the other Sisters."

My brows furrowed. Could he be implying what it seemed? "You mean...you were improper with her?"

He glanced at me sharply, and much of the love I'd felt seemed to vanish. "Was I? *I?*"

"But...you just seemed to say..."

"Whose choice was it to make me go to her chambers? Who always pulled me away with imperious demands?"

"I'm sorry, Thomas, I guess I didn't mean...but, you kept coming here...you mean she was forcing you, somehow?"

He barked a bitter laugh. "Yes, I kept coming. What, do you think I told the villagers what she was doing? If possible, they held her in more awe than you. Could I help it that they continued to send me?" He shook his head. "I don't doubt one of the letters I brought back from Sister Judith requested they do just that."

"But why couldn't you stop her? Are you..." I wasn't sure how to say it. But I had to know. "Did the two of you ever..."

He looked away again. "I don't know all your rules," he said quietly. "Maybe you think we did. She was very careful to make it sound like we didn't, that she remained pure for her vocation."

I tried to think, but everything was tangled. "Could she...have been with child?"

He shook his head. It helped some to know that, and yet...

"I don't understand," I lamented. This was somehow worse than anything I could have imagined. "Why didn't you just stay away?"

He drew a breath, trapped me in his gaze. "Why didn't I," he said. "I've asked myself that so many times. Just make it stop by never being here. Maybe I hoped she would finally get caught, or she would stop of her own volition. I hoped..." He trailed off, and his gaze went down to my hand. I saw his fingers wiggle, his hand inch toward mine and stop short. "I hoped..." he muttered again. His glance came up. He pulled his hand away, crossed his arms as he hunched over himself. "Silly, I guess," he said, a bitter edge to his voice. "You're going to be a Sister." He sniffled in the cold air.

I felt something harden inside me. "Thomas," I said, as gently as I could. "I made you a promise, earlier. Forgive me for not understanding." He glanced at me, still doubting. "I don't know a lot about how things are between men and women, but...from the warnings I've been told, only men are able to force themselves...I mean, you never hear of it going the other way."

He straightened a little. "It is far easier for a man to force himself suddenly," he said. "That's why you hear about it, I suppose. And I suppose Our Father has made us differently—or perhaps The Liar has twisted us differently from the path Our Father would have us walk. I think that's how she did it," he continued, musing now. "By the time she truly began, she had laid groundwork for weeks. And she made it seem like it was what I would want. I regret, Rae-Anna, that I thought I did want it—for a time. You were so distant, so unattainable, so...." He paused, his features softening. "So beautiful, but so remote. Even if you were in the village, I would not be worthy of your spirit. Not at first, and surely someone else would've—" He cut off, shaking his head. "I see you believe it too," he said.

"Not the parts concerning me," I said softly.

He grunted. "Well, with those and so many other words she convinced me I couldn't have you even if I wanted you, or you were free from oaths. But she knew the intricacies of their laws, she said, could find ways around and through them. She grew bolder, and eventually too greedy. I knew she was wrong, knew she had not changed my mind. But by then it was too late. She changed from winsomeness and flattery to condemnation. What would you think of me if you found out what we had done? And she promised to tell you if I tried to get free."

"All those times these past several days you came, I thought I saw shame in some of your glances, but directed at me," I said. It made much more sense, now, his reactions when Sister Judith came around. The hardness I felt in me grew in size and in heat as I contemplated it.

"I had determined, finally, to come out with it," he said. "Last time I came. I wanted to give you something, to hopefully soften the blow and convince you I was in earnest. I told her I was done. I thought she accepted it. I thought maybe finally she had changed—maybe because of what was happening to you. She promised she would give you the gift, that it would be better to do that first, to soften your heart toward me—" He cut off as my gaze hardened. I was positively gazing daggers at him, though they weren't meant for him.

"A necklace?" I asked. "With a blue stone?"

He swallowed quickly and nodded.

My fist tightened on the bench. I knew the flames were there, but I didn't care. She dared hide behind the veil, to use her power and influence, to take up the mantle of The Beloved for such despicable, depraved ends.

I felt the flames grow hot, hotter than ever before—it didn't burn me, it was just the sense. But now Thomas was rising urgently. His mouth moved but I didn't hear him as the flames roared:

For our God is a consuming fire!

Chapter 10

Thomas finally succeeded in pulling me to my feet and away from the bench as it burned. A small part of me registered it, but the fire still raged in my hand and the anger still raged in me. "She stole it, Thomas," I said. "We found the necklace on her after she burned to death. She probably was going to tell you I had rejected it, rejected you."

"And that made you so angry?" he asked. "That I might think you rejected me?"

The fire damped, and I looked softly at him. "Not entirely," I said. "*That* I think would make me sad and confused. No, this anger is how she abused The Beloved, using reverence for him as a means of power. She seemed to long have forgotten his abjection on the cross. I pray this has not murdered your view of The Beloved or Our Father."

He nodded. "For a time it did," he said. "A long time. But I think, as you say, I knew it was her own will. Certainly no words from the pulpit portrayed such a life for us or of The Beloved."

"And no one knew of what was happening?" I asked, a new thought chilling my heart. "None of the Sisters here?"

His emphatic shake comforted me. "I think not. Obviously, I cannot know for certain. But surely none of the other Sisters here had fallen so far too?"

My suspicions came back. "They knew she was doing something wrong, knew they should have expelled her some time ago. For what, they refuse to tell me."

His gaze hardened as well. "Is that what you didn't want to tell me earlier?" I nodded. "I can understand, I guess. Perhaps they acted in ignorance, but..." He shook his head. "But if they had, I would have suffered so much less."

I looked aside as the bench finally collapsed in its burning heap. The dead and dry ground kept the fire from spreading, and it looked now like a simple cooking fire. Different names for different fires. It had certainly destroyed in its time, and comforted in other times. And it said "*our* God."

"I don't know why things worked out the way they did," I said. "Far more suffering than ours has been permitted to continue, far before our lifetimes—and from outside and inside the house of Our Father."

"You mean...the men below," he said quietly. I nodded. He took a deep breath. "That's what I came to tell the Sisters," he said. "The men returned this morning. It seems the goal of their journey will not go unmet."

"What is the goal?" I asked, aghast.

"They intend to visit the graves—they refuse to say why."

"You have to stop them!"

"How? It breaks no law to visit a gravesite, no matter who is interred. Some of the men have made attempts to...dissuade them—and they seem to take us seriously. But I've seen their eyes. They won't be deterred. I wanted to warn the Sisters, warn you, that they may come seeking entrance."

"Will they harm us?" I asked it benignly. Logically I should have been terrified, and a few days ago I would have been. I was less scared than I was disgusted that there could be men who were undeterred from visiting such an unholy place. Unless... "What do you think their intentions are? Do they come to pay some sort of honor; or might they come to destroy the graves entirely?"

Thomas made to speak, then stopped as he considered. "I have not seen much of them. Glimpses between the village councilmen. They could be as you say, but..." He trailed off, then shook his head.

"What are we to do?"

"Sister Lucy has agreed that if some danger threatens, someone will ring the bells...vigorously." He grinned. "And we will have men ready to ride to your aid." He sobered suddenly. "And hopefully we will not be too late."

I laid a hand on his arm. "There are bolt-holes aplenty in this convent; most of us will be able to hide, I think."

He smiled. "I must return home," he said. "Lots of work to do. I'll let you know when the men have gone, and we can hopefully move past all this."

I nodded, but his words were more complicated than he might have realized. The cloying was still there; the fire had not come just to cleanse the convent of Judith (I hesitated to call her "Sister" anymore) and burn a bench down. I might have to answer for that too. But if the fire remained, there must be more work to do. And I agreed with Thomas: the men wouldn't be deterred, and I feared the fire remained in order to deal with whatever was going on with the evil men buried below.

As Thomas departed, the bells rang Lentus. I ran to the kitchens, very late, but Sister Bethenny only eyed me. The noon meal was nearly prepared, but there were dishes ready for cleaning and I set to.

After prayers and our noon meal I raced back to the kitchens. Sister Lucy was there and she held up a hand to slow my career. I clasped my hands and lowered my head. Act like a Sister.

"You spoke to Thomas?" she asked. I nodded. "What did he tell you?"

"He told me the strange men in the village had returned, and would not be sent away; that we should be ready."

"Fear not those men, daughter; Our Father protects us all, and can certainly keep us safe from a few ruffians."

"The way He protected Thomas?" I asked, trying but failing to keep the bitterness from my voice. The hardness returned, and I couldn't keep from opening my mouth. "Or the way He protected Judith?"

Sister Lucy tsked and made a slashing motion with her hand. "Do you condemn us all so easily?"

I set my jaw and looked up. "I only ask the question, Sister; the condemnation is yours to decide."

"And do you feel yourself worthy of asking such questions? Perhaps we honor you too quickly with the name daughter."

I kneaded the hardness inside, took a breath to soften it. It yielded little. "I do not know what I am worth, Sister," I said. "Perhaps I am as worthless as Judith told me over and over again. As worthless as I told myself—worthless except as a danger to the Sisters and this convent. Do you know I nearly threw myself from the bell tower? I thought this fire was a curse, that I was possessed by many demons and the only way to protect all of you was to go to the Abyss and hopefully take them with me. Our Father stepped in, made me by happenstance read a strange passage from His Words. My curiosity over their meaning overwhelmed my desire for suicide, and by seeking the truth I came unknowingly to the moment of ridding this convent of a true passage of demonic evil. Perhaps I am worth less to you and the other Sisters. But I seem—despite my efforts—worth plenty to Our Father. Ask Him."

Sister Lucy gawked a moment, seemed on the verge of tears. She clamped her jaw shut and strode past me, cloak swirling. I did not watch her go, but went to the scullery to attend my task.

It gave me no joy to speak that way. Sister Lucy had always been the kindest to me. And yet she had harbored Judith—her and the rest of the Sisters—nearly destroying myself and Thomas, and who knows who else, in the process. I couldn't help but feel if she truly cared about me, if any of them did, they would have dealt more harshly with the known evil. Better that than concern themselves that I was left handed.

Perhaps they didn't know about Thomas. But by Sister Bethenny's own admission they knew *something* was wrong. Had wanted to be rid of Judith and yet hadn't. I felt a tiny pang of remorse, now; I did not yet know the whole story. I meant not to pass judgement—I truly believe my heart did not. I only asked the questions, as I had said to Sister Lucy; if their hearts condemned them, that was theirs to handle.

As I scrubbed, it seemed the cloying I had noticed in the morning worsened. I looked up from the large kettle I scrubbed and sniffed. Not worse; real. Before it had been a sense, something more in my thoughts and not actually stimulating my nose. Now, though, it was a definite smell.

A fear struck me: Sister Penelope thought the fire was something outworldly, but was entering more and more into our world. Couldn't this cloying be some outworldly evil? I thought perhaps the fire would come to defend us—hoped for it, prayed for it. But it did not. Yet there came a sense of calm...no, understanding. As when a child fears a noise but the parent knows, and does not fear. Except I didn't know what it was—did I?

I stood, away from the dirty water. It seemed familiar. Maybe I was jumping at shadows. Ignoring the bizarre turn my world had taken, I sniffed again. When it came to me, I nearly had to laugh at myself.

A dead rat—or some small creature. Nothing evil or strange. I began searching for it to dispose of it outside the walls.

But then my searching gaze fell on the rasped-out lettering on the shelf, now obscured further by the pots and pans I had cleaned so far. The bizarreness came back; the rats were not as innocent as they had once been. The other cloying, the one that seemed supernatural, was still present. I thought I should get another Sister, just in case.

But even as my feet turned for the stairway, I stopped. I had the fire; it would surely protect me. I resumed my search.

Finally, deep in a far corner, I found it. It was bedraggled, as though it had drowned some time ago and mostly dried. I didn't know how it would have gotten there, though. I moved an urn out of the way so I could reach it better. What had killed it eluded me; as I said it looked almost drowned, except it couldn't have gotten to that corner if it had. I couldn't imagine anything dragging it that far and no further.

I prodded it with my toe. Definitely very stiff. It slid with the sound of dried leaves on the stone. Even the tail remained curled just so, as if the whole carcass were desiccated. So where did the drowned look come from?

As I inspected the corner, I noticed a dark stain. I backed away into better light, then gasped. The toe of my slipper was red with blood—or was it just clay, again? I couldn't seem to trust my own mind anymore. I prayed again for the fire; this time, no peace or understanding came.

I heard a shuffle upstairs. "Sister Bethenny?" I called.

"Yes, daughter," came back, slightly muffled.

"Could you come down here, please?"

She did not hurry, but she came, brows raised and only the faintest look of impatience.

"I'm sorry, Sister, but sometimes I don't know if I can trust my eyes. Is that blood? Or just very red clay?"

She looked where I pointed, cocked her head. "It is the reddest clay I've perhaps ever seen, daughter, but it isn't blood. Where did it come from?"

I gestured. "I found a dead rat, in the corner here, and pushed it with my toe to make sure it was dead. With all the strange things happening lately, I didn't want to leave. I'm sorry to bother you."

She waved me off. "I understand, daughter," she said. "I forgot for a moment, but you were right to take caution." She turned, going back up the stairs. "You are going to get rid of that rat, yes?"

"Of course, Sister." I turned back, not fully appeased. Even if it was the reddest clay—and it still looked entirely like blood to me—it still followed that the rat must have been deep in the catacombs where I had last encountered a blood-red clay. And nothing from down there could be trusted.

Apologizing silently, I took a pair of tongs from its rack and grasped the rat by the tail. When I lifted it, I heard a faint *pat, pat, pat* as the blood clay dripped off of it. That wouldn't do; I could not drip even clay all through the convent. I glanced around, settling on a small pot. I held it under the rat as it became a *ting, ting, ting* of dripping into the bottom.

Quickly I mounted the stairs. Sister Bethenny glanced up as she heard the *ting, ting, ting;* I shrugged apologetically. "It's still dripping," I explained. Her bows furrowed, but I could only shrug again; I didn't know how or why it would be so soaked, either.

I stopped at the door, with no hand free to turn the latch. The *ting, ting, ting* echoed in the silence as I glanced back for help. Sister Bethenny came forward quickly and let me out.

The wind picked up as I hurried along the cloister, my steps faster than the dripping. A bleak sun cast weary shadows. I glanced aside at the burned bench, which I had still not brought to the attention of any of the Sisters. It had chilled, and no wisp of smoke rose from the heap. My brow furrowed a moment—a fire that hot should not have cooled that quickly—but the *ting, ting, ting* brought me back and I hurried for the gate.

Another hurdle, as I still had no hand for a latch. I set the pot on the ground, carefully holding the rat aloft. I suppose I could have just put the rat inside the pot, but something in me didn't want to let go of it with the tongs. I opened the door, turned my back against it, then picked up the pot and hurried on.

Thick clouds were coming, and something in them heralded snow. Perhaps it was just the cold air, and the season. It might have just been idle fancy; the fields stretched out below the convent when they were covered in snow gave me a certain sort of savage beauty. Maybe it was because I had struggled up that slope—weary and starved—several months ago on my way to the convent.

I shook myself back to the present. As I had relaxed in my reverie, I had nearly dipped the rat into the pot. Only the tongs with the tail were still above the rim, the rest of the body hid in the darkness inside.

Ting.

I froze, unconsciously stretching my hands further away from me, waiting for the dripping to resume. I began to lift the rat out, to see if it had just suddenly dried up. I held it in the frozen air, completely stiff, but no longer dripping. I sighed. Jumping at shadows.

It screeched, arching up suddenly and scrabbling at the tongs with its paws. I shrieked, dropping rat, tongs, and pot and stepping quickly away. The stain on my slipper could be nothing other than blood, and it dragged across the ground.

The rat bolted, thankfully away from me, but—terrifyingly—back toward the convent. I scooped up the pot and ran after it, fully intending to bash it over the head if I could. But it had been dead! Completely dead, stiff and everything. I had seen dozens—hundreds—of dead rats in my time. I knew a dead rat when I saw one.

But somehow this one was alive. It reached the convent wall, but blessedly turned alongside it. Curiosity replaced my fear and I followed it. It seemed not to care that I was present—that it wasn't running away from me but toward something. I saw its whiskers twitching as it sniffed the ground.

We circled around to the far side of the convent, then struck off across a bit of open ground. I began to notice the chill through my dress, now, worried about how far away the rat would take me. I would need to figure out how far was too far, before it *became* too far.

The forest was near. I should just catch up, bash its head in, and be done. I did not. We wove between the trunks. Ahead of us there were the fallen timbers where the thunderbolts must have struck during that terrible storm nearly two weeks ago—and where, I realized in horror, the ground must have caved in over the catacombs.

This horror slowed me, and the rat scampered with renewed energy. Before I could stop it, it reached the edge of the rended ground and scurried down into the hole. I stopped at the edge, afraid to go on, afraid it would collapse further and draw me in. There was only a broken darkness below; the light did not extend far enough to see if it opened into the actual catacombs.

I turned to go, and saw it: a footprint, not my own, but of a heavy boot, pointing toward the village.

Chapter 11

I was no tracker. I had known men who could do it, from the village, and knew the principles. But I could not locate another print. Maybe only the ground near the cave-in had been soft enough. Maybe someone else would have been able to see a sign. But the fact it had been there was worrying enough.

Perhaps the strange men Thomas kept telling me about had found the spot. Had finally found a way to access the catacombs without bothering with permission from the Sisters. It seemed a terrible coincidence that the spot *right above* those evil men had been the spot to collapse. But it also seemed odd to me there was only one print, and it pointed away from the cave-in and toward the village. Surely there should have been at least one pointing *toward* the hole, from whomever had come upon it to begin with. My footprints littered the ground as I continued to search for some clue, some other sign.

I gave up. I was no tracker. I dared not descend into the catacombs after the rat. I turned back toward the convent. I wasn't exactly sure how I was going to report this to Sister Lucy, but she needed to know.

I still worried if she would believe me. Maybe I worried she would be angry with me for how I had spoken to her earlier. Spiteful. I felt like I would be, if our places were switched. But she had been my greatest ally until recently. And she was in charge until Mother Superior returned.

I looked up suddenly, just as the bells began to ring. It was not the hour for prayer. Were they ringing...vigorously? Sounding an alarm? It sounded as though they were trying to get someone's attention but...

Then I was able to see down the road toward the village, saw a small pack train winding its way toward the convent. Third from the front was Mother Superior. She had returned.

"Oh, no," I said aloud, hitching up my skirts as I began to run. I had forgotten entirely that she was due back today, and I was in no condition to welcome her. She would be given a fair amount of pomp on her return. We did not always do so, but it had been her longest time away since I had arrived. Even when I still lived in the village, we knew she was never gone for more than a day or two. I still had not been told her entire reason for being gone so long this time. Some council, supposedly.

Not that it mattered. She was returned, and my dress and shoes were filthy and my hair unbound. I ran through the chill afternoon air as the bells faded away. As I rounded the corner of the convent I slowed, knowing she would see me anyway. She would know I was the only acolyte here and know that I had probably been somewhere I shouldn't. She wouldn't know what had gone on here the past week—unless the villagers told her, but even they knew little. I wondered how she would respond. Not just to me, but to the news. How Sister Lucy might break it to her. *When* Sister Lucy might break it to her. I half expected Sister Lucy to come running out any moment.

But of course, that wasn't her way.

My heart dropped again when I saw the gate was still open as I had left it. I had meant only to dispose of the rat and come back; now I had been gone the larger part of half an hour. All was quiet and normal when I slipped in and shut the door. As I made my way toward my cell to straighten up, Sister Bethenny rounded a corner and caught sight of me.

"Where have you been? Where is my cookware?"

I gaped like a landed fish. "Oh, um, it's uh..."

She waved me off. "You'll answer later. Get ready for the Mother Superior. Hurry."

I veered off course, went to the washroom first and tried to scrub my face and hands. My face cleaned up okay, but I felt like rat-dander stuck to my hands. I still couldn't understand how a thing that seemed so dead had come so quickly back to life. I was nearly becoming accustomed to the incomprehensible.

I also wetted my hair to try to make it easier to brush. I could almost feel a headache coming on from the cold, but it was somewhat my fault. I toweled it lightly then went to my cell.

There was little I could do about my dress, and fortunately it didn't show too much dirt. Still, I took it off and set it aside as I brushed my hair, then beat it lightly with my hands and smoothed it as best I could. I had barely slipped it over my head when I heard the gate bell clanging.

I was supposed to have been there already, opening it instantly on their call. Instead I sprinted through the garden, picturing their quizzical glances as the door remained fast. The only way to make it worse would be to call out that I was coming, so of course I did that.

All the Sisters of the convent were in a line near the door, and every head turned toward me, a spectrum of looks from quizzical to consternation. I can only imagine Mother Superior's true thoughts as a red-faced and panting acolyte a few months away from possibly taking the vows opened the door to her and her entourage.

Her face was, of course, serene. Maybe a little bit of mirth behind her eyes? Surely not. I looked down, backing away with my hands folded demurely. "Welcome back, Mother," I said belatedly.

"Thank you, child," she said, no tinge of condemnation or anger in her voice. She seemed...happy. She had done so before—she was rarely a stern Mother—but even so it felt out of place.

Sister Lucy stepped forward. "Mother," she said, bending quickly to kiss her outstretched hand. Mother Superior laid a hand on Lucy's head. "Thank you, daughter," she said. Now, I could hear a note of concern in her voice. We all did.

"Much has happened while you were away, Mother," Sister Lucy said as she straightened, knowing Mother Superior noticed Judith's absence. "We are in the midst of very strange times—deep in the midst. We should speak immediately."

"I had some sense of it, coming through the village," she replied. "And yet it still was cloaked mostly in shadows and guesses. Are we under threat?"

"I believe some, Mother, though..." She trailed off and shook her head. "I cannot say how much, or how dire. I'm afraid these times escape any wisdom I thought I had gained."

"Well," Mother said with a gusty sigh. "Let's see what counsel can untangle. I had hoped to shake off some dust from the road but your looks tell me that should wait. Child, please help get these books and things to my quarters."

"Actually, she should be there as well, Mother," Sister Lucy said, bowing her head again. "She seems somewhat at the center of what's been happening."

Mother Superior appraised me with a lifted eyebrow. "Is she indeed? As the cause?"

I swallowed hard, afraid to hear how Sister Lucy would respond, fearing still her spite. It pained enough to hear from Mother Superior's own mouth the same prejudice resurfacing that had chased me from the village in the first place.

"That may take further untangling," Sister Lucy said. I glanced up to see her expression toward me cool. "I would say no, at least not by her will."

I planted my gaze firmly on the ground. I could tell by her tone she would not want to see my gratitude until Mother Superior had decided for herself.

"Well," said Mother, "let me hear unfettered talk first. Help take these things to my quarters, child, and then join us in the Chapterhouse."

"Yes, Mother."

Mother and the Sisters left in a swirl of cloaks as I turned to the mule train. The men had already unloaded many of the smaller boxes, and two of the mules had been for provender and would not be unloaded. There remained only two larger boxes, each of which apparently took all four men to hold in place as they untied it.

"What are those?" I couldn't help but ask. One man—dark complected with a thick but close-cropped beard—glanced my way.

"We ask not what is the lady's," he said in a thick accent I had never heard before. Not that many foreigners ever came through Holden. I found my attention strangely attracted to it.

"Where are you from?" I asked. Part of me knew I should be simply going quietly about Mother Superior's orders, and yet...

The final strap came loose, and the dark man and the other one stepped quickly away as the other two strained to lower the box to the ground. They all seemed curiously intent on ignoring me, except the dark man.

He again spared me only a glance. "Algiers," he said quickly. All four again set-to, the mule protesting the unbalanced weight.

I hesitated. "You're a Moor?" I had heard enough about them that I couldn't imagine Mother Superior bringing one of those in her train.

Again his dark glance glittered. "Born, yes." He paused, grunting as they struggled a moment with the heavy box. "I cannot help that."

"I'm sorry," I said quickly. As if I hadn't faced the same judgement. Whatever curiosity I had fled, and I turned quickly to pick up some of the smaller boxes.

"I am Mahmoud," he said. I turned to him. "And you are forgiven."

We stood silently facing each other as the other three men busied themselves with the other cargo. "Rae-Anna," I said finally. "And, thank you."

He bowed slightly before turning to help his compatriots. I turned away and hurried to Mother Superior's quarters with my armload.

When I finished, I went to the Chapterhouse and entered quietly. Sister Lucy was in the midst of relating the events after I had awoken with the fire inside me, approaching the point of my judgement. Mother Superior glanced at me as I stood to the side, motioning me forward as she returned her attention to Sister Lucy.

"We of course discussed punishment or penance among us, but could come to no consensus. Sister Judith finally prevailed."

"She was known to do that," Mother Superior replied heavily. "And the decision?"

As Sister Lucy told it, I could see Mother Superior's gaze darkening. When she got to the part about the bell, Mother Superior cut her off.

"Faugh! A bell? Truly? And you all allowed it?"

"It seemed...excessive, Mother, and yet...the danger..."

Mother Superior cast me an incredulous glance. "This child?"

"Not her, Mother; the fire," Sister Lucy said, her tone pleading. I assumed I would be on trial, and it seemed much more like the rest of the Sisters were. I wasn't sure how to take it, so I sat as demurely as I could while still observing.

"Yes, I will need to see this fire," she muttered. She glanced at me, and I could tell she somehow knew it might not come on command. Maybe they had already told her that part. She sighed. "Continue."

Sister Lucy did, the other Sisters chiming in when it was their turn. Mother Superior asked thorough questions, turning out every fault, misstep, and preconceived notion along the way. She did, as well, point out when wise action was taken.

"As to the demise of Sister Judith," Sister Lucy said, "perhaps Rae-Anna should tell that part."

I swallowed. Chairs creaked as every eye and every body shifted toward me. I had not prepared in the slightest for this moment.

Take no thought how or what ye shall speak; for it shall be given you in that same hour.

There was a gasp, and Mother Superior's eyes goggled. I held my hand away from me; the fire this time was not as fierce as it had been the last few times. Just a gentle burning. But I wasn't sure if it would still ignite anything I touched.

"This is the fire," I said, bizarrely calm, as though simply introducing a friend. And yet, it didn't seem that bizarre once I thought it. It *had* been a friend, many times. Just sometimes a very wrathful and violent friend.

It dimmed further, and I felt it was safe to hold my hands in my lap again. "If I might be allowed, Mother, it is difficult to understand what happened in the cellar with Sister Judith without telling you

my story from the start—from when I became lost in the catacombs."
She gestured assent, and I began. It came out easily, I thought, and
Mother Superior asked far fewer questions. There were plenty of
missteps, to be sure, and few instances of wise action. I did feel a
slight pang of guilt as I knew I was telling things that I had neglected
to tell Sister Lucy or any of the others. I pointed out that fact in their
defense. Mother Superior's face darkened.

"You lied," she said. "In the face of this strange and fearful thing,
a thing to rightfully terrify those who would be your Sisters, you held
back. One might wonder why."

"I was scared, Mother," I whispered.

"Of course you were! I expect nothing less. But fear must drive you
further into the arms of The Beloved, not away from them."

"I was afraid I would be put out of the Convent. Afraid I would be
thrust from the arms of The Beloved against my will. Afraid I was
never in them to begin with."

Her eyes glittered. "We'll see," she said. "Tell me about the cellars."

I continued, leaving nothing out. A change came over her as I told
her of the rats' writing and Judith's death—a closing off. I feared I
had lost my argument, somehow, despite telling the truth.

"After that, several Sisters indicated...well, that maybe I was less
at fault." The words that had flowed so easily before seemed to get
caught up on my tongue now. "I mean, that there was something
wrong with Jud—Sister Judith...or...and, well Thomas told me—"

Mother Superior cut me off. "That's enough, child. It concerns
me greatly that the rats somehow acknowledged you—or that some
power that influenced the rats acknowledged this fire. And, of
course, that it seems now able to burn and destroy."

"It's not doing it now, though," I said quickly, glancing down at my
hand. But the fire had departed. "Well, it didn't," I added, looking up.

"I would rather it acted consistently," Mother Superior replied. "How do we know that next time it won't burn again?"

"The things it says to me," I said, becoming desperate. "Sometimes sound so familiar..." I trailed off as she stared at me.

"Of course they are familiar, child," she said. "They are the words of Our Father. We read from them every day."

Several things came to me at once: firstly that they were, of course, from the Holy Words, which was why the Parable of the Tares also sounded familiar; secondly, that I had not heard the words read aloud since Sister Judith had taken over in Mother Superior's absence; and thirdly, that the cloying I had thought I smelled earlier, before the dead-undead rat, was back a hundred-fold.

The rest of the Sisters and Mother Superior smelled it, too, and we all glanced at each other with wrinkled noses. Mother Superior grew red in the face. "Daughters, surely none of you, at such a time..."

We all denied it emphatically. The smell became overpowering, now a rotting stench. Then I heard a faint clattering, reminding me of dead leaves blowing across the gardens, but they would not have been so loud. But it was a sound definitely like dried bones rattling against one another.

Chapter 12

We fled to the gardens, hoping for fresh air. When we arrived, we found the gate still open, the donkeys standing dutifully by, and Mahmoud on the ground clutching a wound.

"What happened here?" Mother Superior demanded, striding to him.

"Those men you hired," he said through gritted teeth. "They refused to come back with me, drawing blades against me when I insisted."

"Where did they go?"

Mahmoud's head thumped against the ground. "Inside," he said. "I did not see where. One said something of your catacombs, of answering a call."

Mother Superior rounded on me. "Many have heard that call, it seems," she said. "You have brought these men here, no doubt. Afraid of being thrown out, you said? Before you could accomplish your purpose?"

"Mother!" I said, eyes burning. "I have done nothing but love

The Beloved since I arrived. Ask the Sisters how I undertook my penance!"

"Oh, I am certain," she responded, eyes dark. "Those bent on evil undertake many things."

"As do those bent on righteousness," I offered timidly.

"I think not, *Lord of Fire*," she spat. "Daughters, let us go. We have evil to rid from our convent."

"Men with swords?" Sister Bethenny asked.

"They may come with swords, but we come in the name of Our Father and Beloved," Mother Superior said. Without waiting for further dissent she strode through the gate, the Sisters hesitantly behind her. Sister Lucy went last, casting me a glance of resignation and shame. The gate boomed shut, leaving me and Mahmoud outside.

"Friendly women," Mahmoud muttered. "I suppose you are not a doctor?" I looked at him helplessly. He grinned tightly, his face beginning to pale. "Ah. I wonder what my fault was."

"They're afraid," I said, kneeling beside him. "Fear isn't concerned with fault, only safety."

"So they run at swords with crosses?"

I shrugged. "A sword is just another type of cross, isn't it? Just pointier."

His eyes searched mine, and he coughed a laugh when he got the joke. "If only they had struck deeper, or not at all, with their pointy things," he said.

The cloying, nearly gone in the gardens, began to waft on the winds. And the bone-clatter came occasionally, faintly. "They come for me," he whispered.

"Who?" I asked.

"The dead. Come to receive me."

A fear began to grow that he was closer to the truth than he knew.

And the Sisters and Mother were inside alone. I wasn't entirely sure how I could help, except...

The fire came to my hand, just then, and I wondered. Was Mother Superior correct? The fire had first come from the crypts, as if it sought out the same men those three murderers now also sought. The rats had bowed to me as wielder of the fire. I had killed, and burnt to ash; I had lied. I thought I had not *meant* any of those things, but did I truly know my own heart? Even an imbecile held some culpability.

Mahmoud shifted, and I saw him staring at the flames. "It's you," he whispered hoarsely.

"What's me?" I asked.

"The wielder of fire." His dark eyes fixed on me, and I saw a terror flickering within. "I did not think it would be...but you are here." He sagged, wracked with a fit of coughing. "And I nearly dead."

"How did you know about me?"

He was ashen, now, his tunic and the ground beneath him soaked. "I did not think it would be as I died," he continued as if I had not spoken. "A shame. But there is hope still. It comes now, the winnowing fork. A bad day to be chaff," he said with another coughing laugh.

With his stripes, we are healed.

I looked at Mahmoud's wound. I had seen the doctor in the village, once, using hot iron to cauterize a wound. I prayed I had not heard wrong as I laid my hand on Mahmoud's bleeding flesh. I felt the fire like a narrow blade slide into his wound and draw along it.

He gasped, cried out, writhing. I nearly removed my hand, except the wounded man in the village had done much the same. I continued to pray, searching my heart.

The fire winked out, and Mahmoud collapsed, gasping. His

breaths seemed easier, and far deeper than he'd been able to draw previously. His skin was still sallow—but, it was not as though the blood he had lost would have returned to his body. His dark eyes, still pained, gazed at me.

"*Mashallah.*"

I thought he thanked me. "The Beloved instructed me to, though I did wish it," I said. And it presented another thorny problem: now the fire displayed healing as well, something demons never did. But surely if it were something righteous, the Sisters would have known! Who better than they, devoting their whole lives to one whom I had only begun to know recently? And yet, my faith in them was quickly eroding.

A footstep crunched behind me and I spun, hand raised. Thomas took a quick step back, hand before him. His other was on the hilt of a sword at his waist.

"Oh, Thomas," I said, standing quickly and falling into his arms. He seemed hesitant at first, then gave in and held me. All my tumbled thoughts came out through my tears on his shoulder. Despite the nearness of The Beloved and the sometimes-comforting words of this strange fire, there was still something about Thomas' physical presence, his ability to hold me with arms of flesh and bone, the reality of him, that I longed for.

After some moments I backed away, wiping my eyes with a sleeve. "Thank you," I said—for simply accepting me without demanding more, I didn't say.

His eyes searched mine for a moment, then turned to Mahmoud. "Who is this?" he asked.

"Mahmoud," I replied, turning. "And this is Thomas. Mahmoud came with Mother Superior, to help with her baggage train." I continued, briefly telling Thomas the rest of the story. "But why are you here? And why do you have a sword?" I asked.

"Pyotr," he said darkly. "I wish the man paid more attention."

"I don't understand."

"He had a gift prepared for Mother Superior, things to keep you through the winters. But it was too much for her and—Mahmoud, I guess—to handle, so he gave her three helpers."

"Yes, they were the ones who stabbed him!" I said. As soon as the words left my mouth, connecting with what Thomas was saying, I blanched.

"I'm not surprised. They were three of those looking to visit the crypts."

My hand flew to my mouth, but it was from within the convent that the scream came. We all turned, though we would see nothing over the walls. There were several other shrieks and muffled shouts, then a door crashing shut and scattering footsteps.

"What's happening?" I shouted. "Let us in!"

I saw shadows bolting past windows up the stairwell into the dormitories I had cleaned. One figure at the end moved slower, seemed to be walking backward. It had to be Mother Superior, and I thought she was sprinkling holy water behind her.

Finally Sister Lucy paused and leaned out a window as the other Sisters continued by her. "Begone!" she shouted. "We wouldn't let you in if we could, cursed child! No doubt this is your fault—it's all clear! Sister Judith held this at bay, until you removed her. We were wrong! And now Sister Aitrinn has paid the ultimate price. So go!"

I stood in shock. Sister Lucy, always a friend, turned so completely against me. What could be happening in there? Why was the rotting smell so strong, now? Where once had been footsteps there now rose again the clattering of bones. But there was no more shouting; it was eerily silent besides.

Thomas ran forward and threw himself against the door, and bounced back. "You won't get through that way," I said absently. I knew how heavily barred the other side was. So long we had all fought against this fire because we didn't understand it. Had barely even tried to, at least at first. And yet it had just healed a man.

Whatever was happening, we needed to raise the alarm. If we could ring the bell—the Sisters were apparently barricading themselves in the dorms, and would not be able to get to it—the men of the village would come. But they would need a way inside.

"We have to get in there," I said.

Thomas looked at me. "I wish I had thought that," he said.

I spared him a withering glance. Then I needed to take a deep breath. I felt the nudging of the fire—it yearned to be inside the convent, somehow let me know that was why it had come. And there was only one way in that I knew.

"If we can get the men from the village to come, it might help. But we'll need to open the door for them. I know how to get inside." I shuddered once, then turned. "Come with me. Mahmoud, will you be okay to stay here?"

He nodded, his skin looking ruddier now, and he managed to pull himself into a little higher sitting position. I led Thomas at a quick pace around the back side of the convent toward the woods, toward the gaping hole that I knew was above the catacombs. The wind was still, and the stench faded away now. Each step became firmer. I couldn't fathom it, but the Sisters were wrong. And it was not my heart that was right—or, to the extent it was, it was only because the wisdom of the fire, the revelation of Our Father's Words impressed upon me. I trusted not so much myself as Him, as revealed through the Words. I didn't know what had happened to the faith of the Sisters, but that was not for me to decide. All I could do was as I was led. And I was led again to the catacombs.

"Are you sure about this?" Thomas asked as he peered into the hole.

"Not even a little bit," I said. "But I believe."

Thomas took a deep breath, drew his sword, and slithered his way down into the hole. I heard a thud, and a grunt, and then a clattering of stone before there was silence. My heart hammered as the moments dragged on.

"Are you coming?" he asked finally.

"Oh, sorry; I was waiting for you to tell me it was safe."

"I don't know about that, but at least the fall won't kill you."

I snorted, then gripped my skirts and slid into the hole. It went pitch-dark very quickly, and suddenly the firmness of the earth gave way to thin air. I sucked in a breath a moment before I hit flesh; Thomas caught me, and set me down on my feet.

"Thanks," I said shakily. Now I was down here, and my eyes had adjusted, the light from above was enough to give some shape to the shadows. I saw the broken stones that had been limned by the fire, but there was now even more clutter than before. I gasped again.

There were four bodies on the floor, mutilated beyond recognition. Three were missing heads and hands and looked...fresher. I recognized them from above. The fourth I had never seen and was missing his feet and half of his chest, and his blood had dried. The four sarcophagi of the men from Holden were shattered open and empty.

"What have they done?" I whispered.

"I was hoping you could tell me," Thomas said.

I forced my mind to think. Away from the grisly horror before me I might have made the connection sooner. "It's...they...oh, Our Father and Beloved..." My knees nearly failed me. "They gave the parts that the Brothers were missing. As punishment, the Brothers had been buried without head and hands, and Bruce without feet and left ribs. They must have..." I trailed off, not sure what they must have done. Then I remembered the rat. "Surely..." Thomas and I locked gazes. "They must have raised them from the dead," I said.

Thomas' flat stare rebuked me, but it made some sense. As much sense as anything else made these days. "This one came first, not long after the storm. That's why he's stiffer. Then these three came with Mahmoud just now." Thomas looked skeptical. I think I was too. And yet my mind kept working through it. "The rats," I said suddenly, my eyes bright on him. "From the beginning they've seemed...sensitive to what's been happening. Tied up in it—or by it, at least. Earlier today I was carrying a rat that I was sure was dead, and suddenly he was alive and ran to this hole." I gestured to where we had slithered down. "He must have come because of this...whatever it is. Perhaps a call? A call that also brought the three men. Maybe even the same call that trapped me when this all began."

"But what would do such thing?"

"I don't know, Thomas, and the Sisters so far haven't seemed to understand it either. But there is some sort of power at work here."

"But is this it? Just these four? The Sisters didn't seem like they were fleeing from only four men."

I shook my head, fear warring with the courage of the fire. "Come, and let's see," I said.

We made our way through the dim passages, arriving finally to those I knew better, those that were still lit by lamplight. And we were stopped again at the sight of sepulcher after sepulcher broken and emptied—dozens, perhaps a hundred or more.

"If these all are...come to life," Thomas said, fingers flexing on his sword, "I'm not sure how much good this will do."

I shook my head. "We must ring the bell, and get the doors un-barred for the men from the village. We'll try to stay hidden from them until the men arrive."

"I think the bell may draw their attention," he said drily.

I had no response. We made our way along the passage. There were skeletal tracks here and there, and as we moved forward there began to be more full footprints. The stench rose again, I could only imagine then it was the rotting decay of flesh of the more newly-interred. How could someone do this? Why would they?

We made our way up the stairs to the surface, each foot care-fully placed. Above, the large crucifix and bowl of holy water were gone from the sacristy; everything else had been overturned. Once through, I peered through the cracked door to the cloister. We had no way of knowing if any of these things were on the other side or not. All was eerily silent.

I looked out over the cloister. Clouds had come in, and a cold wind rattled a few branches. There were skeletons standing upright in the garden, motionless, all facing various directions. Waiting, it seemed. Watching through hollow, dark sockets. None were armed, at least. But we would not be able to exit without being seen.

I stepped back. "They're out there, watching," I whispered. "We can't leave without them seeing us, and there were maybe ten that I could see that could get between us and the belltower. I'm not sure how quickly they move, but..."

"Are there no other ways out of here?"

I shook my head. "They would only lead further away from the tower."

"Distraction, then," he said, drawing his sword. "I'll go first, lead them away. Once they've moved, you go next."

I wanted to protest, to say something, but he was right. It should have felt like letting go, but he was never mine. Not yet. So I only nodded and moved back behind the door so I would not be seen when he opened it.

It swung without squeaking, but then banged and echoed when it hit the wall. I peeked as he went out, saw ten heads turn toward him—some turned completely around, with no sinews to limit their range—and then ten bodies turned as one and stalked him. They did not run; I wondered if they could not, or didn't feel the need. I waited a few moments, letting them pursue, then stepped out into the doorway.

A shriek deafened me, the hot breath putrid in my face. I stepped back and tripped in the cluttered sacristy. I scrabbled backward as she pursued, and suddenly I was tumbling down the steps back into the catacombs. Sister Aitrinn was above me, limbs twisted. She carried an arm as though the shoulder were ruined, and part of her face was gone. Her eyes were shot through with blood as she moaned, her steps awkward and halting as she pursued me.

I scrabbled to my feet and darted deeper into the catacombs. I prayed Thomas was all right; I wasn't sure how to get to the surface again. I glanced wildly about. On the wall was an unlit torch, there only for those venturing deeper into the catacombs. I grabbed it, taking up a position behind a corner.

I could hear the soft *thump, scrape, thump, scrape* of poor Sister Aitrinn as she hobbled down the corridor. Suddenly, she stopped, a low moan coming from her again. I peeked out; she was perhaps ten paces away, head cocked to the side as if listening.

Just then a piece of broken sarcophagus fell somewhere behind me, and her head snapped to. She saw my eyes, and her jaw opened in another terrible scream as she shuffled rapidly toward me. I ducked back again, waiting. I heard another scrape, saw her foot at the corner, and leapt out swinging.

All the weeks of scrubbing and cleaning and carrying buckets had made me stronger than I realized, as the torch haft took off most of her jaw and smacked her head against the wall. I did not wait to see if I had killed her again or not, and ran back for the exit. I pounded up the stairs and into the daylight.

The cloister was still empty, the garden silent. I made my way along the walk as swiftly and quietly as I could, thankful for the slippers. As I made to pass the hallway to the Sisters' studies, the door to the chapel swung open. I ducked back into the hall, heart hammering, lungs burning as I tried to quiet my breathing.

A skeleton emerged, looking across the garden toward the main gate. In his hand was a tangle of blonde hair. I didn't know whether to run or wait. He hadn't seemed to notice me yet. His jaw clicked as he worked it open; he stepped away, and a swirling breeze began to shut the door. I moved with it, grasping the handle so it did not slam as I shuffled sideways into the chapel.

He turned as if to make for the sacristy, catching sight of me. I ran, sparing only one glance for those gaping sockets. I reached the door to the bell tower and flung it open. He was close behind; it seemed they were able to run if necessary. I pelted up the stairs, nearly dizzy with turning up and up, the sound of bones clattering behind me. I felt a tug on my dress and screamed.

I shot through the trapdoor at the top, slamming it hard behind me. Bones crunched, and four dismembered digits scattered across the wood. I turned and yanked on the bell rope for all I was worth, the shattering clangs echoing across the valley.

Chapter 13

As I pulled I looked out toward the village, hoping to catch some movement, though it was far away. At least I hoped to see when—if—the men were coming. Despite what Thomas had said, I would have understood their desire to stay away.

I caught movement, saw the trapdoor begin to heave open. The skeleton emerged, his jaw set in as clear a snarl as if he'd had lips. I had nowhere to go.

He lunged at me, and I ducked to the other side of the bell as it clanged under its own momentum. We circled back and forth. I felt he got frustrated, though he didn't have the voice to express it. Finally he lunged again, desperately. I circled, leapt for the rope, putting as much of my slight weight into it as I could, trying to bear the whole thing to the ground.

The bell swung mightily, striking him in the ribcage. It didn't shatter, but he stumbled sideways and toppled over the railing. I ran to the edge, watched him shatter on the paving stones below. Two more skeletons were there, and their sockets turned upward. They apprehended me and turned for the door to the chapel.

I only needed to survive until the men got here. If there was just some way to bar the trapdoor! I cast about for anything, even something heavy to slide atop it, but the tower was bare. I had done too good a job in cleaning. I looked at the bell, briefly, but it would be too heavy to move even if I could un-hang it. I was trapped, and I didn't know if I could dispatch two more the way I had the first.

And someone needed to get the main door open, so the villagers could even get inside once they got there. I looked over the wall again; I thought I saw a black mass at the edge of the town, seething as though a hundred men were running. I looked then at the main door and at the empty garden. Where had Thomas gotten to? If he survived, did he plan to come back and get the door? We hadn't really discussed it.

There was clattering on the stairs. I turned, thinking to prepare but having nothing really to do. The trapdoor heaved again, and a skeletal hand emerged, scrabbling on the wooden boards. Then, suddenly, it was yanked back and the door dropped shut. I stood a moment, uncertain; the door heaved again, and a very flesh-covered hand slapped down onto the same boards, and Thomas' head came into view. He was panting, and more than a little dust-covered. I nearly choked when I realized it was probably skeleton dust. I ran to him anyway and hugged him.

"We've still got to get the door open," he said. "Are they coming, the villagers?"

We both turned and looked across the valley. They were indeed drawing nearer, and were much more clearly a host of men with scythes, pitchforks, cudgels, quarterstaffs, and even a few swords. I reached and pulled the rope a few more times to let them know we still lived, though they had no way of knowing what they were coming upon. I also hoped they wouldn't take Mahmoud for an enemy.

"We should get you outside," Thomas said, turning for the trap-door. "Let the men come in and clear out this evil."

I followed, though part of me rebelled. I had done a fair amount to help defeat it, I thought. Was it enough? Was that to be my only role? It was not nothing. I had rung the bell to call reinforcements. And I could not swing a sword. I had done well enough with the torch-haft, but that had been with surprise; once the men came it would likely be a pitched battle against these undead.

But something still nagged at me, some question I couldn't ask or answer. I searched for it as we circled down the flights of stairs. It formed along something like this: why had this all begun? What was it about the men in the crypts that they were able to call others to them, to get them to sacrifice themselves—and what magic caused them to come to life? It was not the sense of life we read of in the Sacred Words, a true life filled with spirit. Sister Aitrinn had come back to animation; these skeletons could move, but they possessed no soul.

I remembered my own call that first day, being drawn in by some compulsion, some strange music, blinded by visions. Was it druid power? Had they woven the magic, and the Brothers somehow tapped into it with their rituals? But I also recalled those dancers, seeming no more in control then I had been, at least at their most frenzied. They and I both were manipulated.

What had changed? Why was I suddenly free of that compulsion? It came again unbidden that perhaps I was still under their compulsion, but I rejected it. Surely they would not have me resist them so forcefully. A house divided could not stand, I thought I had heard.

Unless my resistance was meant only to allow the men to gain access so they could be slaughtered too? I thought about the number of bodies below the convent, how many legions of dead there were on hand.

"Thomas," I said quietly when we reached the bottom. "There are hundreds more below this convent that could be raised to life. Someone should make sure the crypts are empty, and that no others go down there. Or, if they are not empty, how many there are."

He paused, studying me. "I have a sword," he said. "I'll go. But you need to tell the men coming what is happening in here, so they are prepared."

"You can tell them just as well as I," I said. "And I know the catacombs better; I can search it faster and more thoroughly."

"And what happens if you find someone? I still have not seen the four men originally raised; it has only been skeletons and a few with flesh."

"And what of the Sisters?" I asked suddenly.

He shook his head. "They're well-barricaded in the dormitories. The undead seem content to mill about for now."

I furrowed my brow. "What are they waiting for?" My previous thought haunted me: that they were waiting for the village to arrive to slaughter them. I voiced my concern.

Thomas sighed. "I don't know what choice we have," he said heavily. "We cannot let them stay here unchecked, and I don't know if there's a way to seal them inside, at least not permanently. I doubt they can be starved."

So, we had to risk letting the men in and dealing with whatever surprise the undead had. "If only we knew why they were here!" I lamented.

"We need to find Bruce of Holden, and if he's able to speak," Thomas said. "He's probably unhappy about his fate."

I paused, considering. But soon more creaking bones from outside drew our attention. "You have to get the doors," I said again, emphatically. "I'll look in the catacombs. And I promise I'll be careful!"

His hand was on the latch, but he looked at me earnestly. "And what if Bruce is down there? Do you think he'll let you live?"

"The fire defended me against Judith," I said. "If it does not do the same, then it is my fate."

At this he relented, and cracked open the door. I thought I heard shouts, faintly, a roar from the men running for the convent. I worried again for Mahmoud. Thomas exited, giving one last parting glance. I watched him only a moment, saw one skeleton on the far side of the garden turn toward him and begin its stomping walk. It would not reach him in time.

I turned for the catacombs and ran, hurtling through the door and down the steps, praying I would not find Aitrinn waiting for me. The halls were silent but for a faint rush of fire. Orange light wavered on dark walls. I turned cautiously at the corner. At the next turn there was the scuffle and blood from where I had struck Aitrinn, but her body was no longer there. I held my breath a moment, straining my ears to hear any movement. I stepped carefully down the hall. At the turn I retrieved my torch-haft, trying to ignore the bit of gore that still clung to the basket. So armed, I continued deeper.

There were not so many corridors as to be tangled, merely addition after addition. Occasionally, where the rock permitted it, there would be a short loop with a few small alcoves. Mostly there would be a hall, and a room, and a hall, and a room like the string of a rosary. All were empty.

I began to hear chanting, and stopped as I tried to make out the words. They were none I spoke. It sounded like only a few voices, though, and so I pressed on. In truth, I had no idea what I was to do when I found the source; I was not a soldier. The torch-haft was for defense only. And yet I continued, drawing nearer.

I felt the words coil around me and draw tight. I struggled a moment, then was pulled forward, nearly tripping. Somehow I kept my feet as I passed through another room, around another turn. I still held the torch-haft but was sure I would not be able to use it.

The flickering light intensified ahead of me. The chanting grew louder. I was pulled inside the room and stopped: there were five who stood with their backs to me. Aitrinn turned her ruined head, her lower jaw askance but still managing to open in a snarl as jet-black eyes glittered.

My knuckles whitened on the torch-haft and I prayed to be released. But the chanting continued, and the coils around me held me still. Under the chant rose a faint buzz that became a rattling, then a rhythmic pounding. Suddenly, twenty sarcophagi burst, and twenty skeletons crawled out, jaws working. They stood a moment, inspecting themselves and one another as if shocked to be alive. I was shocked, too.

I realized the chanting had stopped. All five were now turned and staring at me. I imagined the four were Bruce and his men. An incredible hate radiated from them all, a loathing of me and what I probably represented to them. From the men it made sense. From Aitrinn I couldn't fathom it: she had been one of the Sisterhood! Had they infected her somehow, shared their hatred when they killed her and then brought her back to life?

"Why are you doing this?" I asked.

"You are a disease," Bruce replied, his voice like a cavalcade of rocks and fire. "Diseases must be cured."

My voice cracked. "*We* are?"

"What right have you to damn a man?" he thundered. "Heaven

and hell are not in your hands, nor the souls of men to direct as you choose. Salvation is not yours to withhold, nor eternal damnation to prosecute."

"Says those who bind with their words, who raise undead, who force the sacrifice of their descendants," I said with not as much energy as I hoped to.

"So we are all evil here," he said, lips cracking as he smiled. "Have you come to join us?"

"Never."

He considered me a long, uncomfortable moment. "Not alive, then," he said quietly. "But as you see, you may join us in death. There is only hatred beyond the grave, when once tasted may never leave the mouth. Even," he gestured to Aitrinn as a joke, "when struck with a torch-haft."

They turned back, beginning their chant again. Aitrinn still faced me, bitterness and rage in her now-obsidian eyes. A low growling came from her throat unbroken, a clicking as it worked past her shattered jaw. She stalked toward me; the bands of the chant still held me.

"Please, Sister, remember yourself," I pleaded. "Remember the livestock you kept and—" I cut off with a yelp as she screamed inarticulate and unholy hatred. I whimpered as she stepped even closer, her face bare inches from mine. Behind her the chanting continued, a buzz and rattle as another detachment of skeletons poised to emerge.

Her eyes darted aside, looking at the torch-haft I still held upraised but immobile. With another sneer she snatched it from my hand, reared back to swing it at my head—retribution for the destruction I had done her.

Instinctively I ducked, and the torch whistled harmlessly overhead. She stared at me in shock; I was able to move. Her surprise turned to alarm, and I felt the familiar presence of fire in my hand. But fear overtook me—fear, and a need to warn the men who had come to save us. I turned and ran.

The chanting faded as I twisted through the passages, but I heard Aitrinn close again on my heels. I glanced back. It was not just her: she led a growing army of skeletons, dozens now, their bleached skulls bobbing in the torchlight as we all ran. There was nowhere to lose them, no way to turn and face them. I was sick with the idea that I led them to the slaughter of the villagers, but I could think of no other course of action.

Orange light faded to white as I neared the stairs to the outside. I felt a brush of air near my head: I think Aitrinn was close enough to swipe at me with the torch-haft as I made for the door. I could hear the rattle of bones, shaking and breaking, thought I heard wooden thumps and the shouts of men. The battle had begun.

I emerged, blinking in the sunlight. A hedge of skeletons and fleshy undead pressed toward the men, whose backs were against the wall. I saw only glimpses of Thomas, sword flashing. Even Mahmoud was there, his scimitar alive in his hands. But they were not winning. Step by step the undead moved forward, and fewer of them fell.

Behind me I heard the scattering of footsteps. I turned, and the new army spread out to cover the cloister. Aitrinn stood vibrating, waiting to move forward, to kill me. Across the way, the noise of battle faded as these unholy reinforcements were perceived. The villagers stopped probably in despair; the skeletons probably because they knew victory was at hand.

I was caught in the middle, surely the first to die. The entire garden stood still as if pausing the moment. Some evil lent the undead a voice and they began a chant, a deep thrum from a hundred skeletal throats. Without pause for breath they repeated the words, a string of them. I began to pick out the various words for "fire" that Sister Penelope had read to me. Their feet began to stomp. At the sound of it, fear washed out like a tide. The words lapped and echoed and swirled and grew louder, throbbing in my ears. Did they somehow still pay me obeisance? Would they listen to the fire? I raised my hand; but, rather than cower, they gnashed their teeth and screamed their words.

As if a command, the troops in front of me began to march forward, Aitrinn leading them with wrath like lightning flashing from her eyes. They stepped from the colonnade, their feet kicking up dust in the once-beautiful garden.

Something inside me settled as I stared at them. My fist tightened by my side and I felt the blue fire turn white-hot.

Chapter 14

Aitrinn did not pause in her stride—perhaps she had no reason to. Even I didn't entirely understand what was happening, though I felt it.

Their chant continued as they marched, as the sound of battle picked up again. But it curled around me, didn't seem to touch me, as I stared down Aitrinn. I didn't know why or how she had turned—but I thought, too, it was not her. Her soul had departed when she died. All that was left was her flesh.

She neared, and I brought my hand to her chest to halt her advance. As it had with Judith, the fire shot into her, seeped in like a sponge, and burned through even faster than it had with Judith. In half a breath her body collapsed in ash.

I think the skeletons did not realize what was among them. Surely they would have paid me more attention. Those in front of me attacked with fists, but not one singled me out specifically. I was still nearly overwhelmed by their sheer numbers.

I danced with the fire, avoiding their grasping hands and swinging

fists, grasping for them myself. Each touch reduced them to ash. The
fire roared and streamed. Bones cracked in the heat. I ran among
them; for every bone I ducked I was able to touch another. Together
we made our way toward the other army.

The wind began to stir, and now clouds of ash swirled in the sky,
nearly choking me. I covered my mouth with one arm, breathing
through my sleeve. The fire flicked like a blade. Sometimes I grasped,
sometimes my palm slid flat, sometimes it was the barest fingertip as
one bony hand tried to parry my arm. To no avail; as long as I could
bring the fire into the least contact with bone or decay, it would go
to work. The chant began to lessen, the intensity slacken as fewer
and fewer undead were able to bring it.

The men on the other side recognized what was happening, or at
least felt the release of pressure. At a roar from Thomas they redou-
bled their efforts. I danced around the back, a blackbird harassing
the hawk, pecking, pecking. The army shifted around me, now; it
had sensed the true threat. They still did not turn to me, but they no
longer disregarded me.

I stumbled in the ash, the ground now slick with it, and fell. One
skeleton, a giant of a man he must have been in life, stepped on the
hand of fire and pinned me to the ground. I wriggled frantically,
trying to get just a finger curled over. He shifted, now stepping firmly
on my forearm; I would not be able to touch him. He leaned over,
that terrible chant still echoing somehow from his empty throat.
He reached down, fingers made longer from lack of a palm curling
around my neck.

I writhed now, flailed with my free hand. He grasped my forearm
calmly with his other hand and squeezed; I felt the bones snap, but
couldn't get a cry through his terrible grip. I stared at him in horror.
The sounds of battle began to fade as darkness closed in. I hoped I

had done enough to give the villagers a chance. I worried that too much time had gone by, that Bruce and his disciples below would have raised countless more already. I closed my eyes.

Something hard struck me in the face and bounced away, and my eyes flew open in shock. The giant still stood on me, but his neck ended in a severed spine. Both of his hands still gripped tightly. But Thomas continued to hack away, bones shattering and spinning away under his blows. Finally I could lift my fire, and I touched the hand at my throat. The fingers burned away and I gasped, then cried out. I touched the other hand, burning it away as well before clutching my broken arm to my chest.

Thomas bent over and picked me up, carrying me away from the garden into the cloister. The chant was gone as the last few clacks scattered away and silence fell. Thomas set me down on a bench and looked me over.

"Are you okay?" he asked.

"Just my arm," I said. "Thomas, more will be coming. Bruce is still down there, he's raising a dozen at a time..."

"The others can worry about that," he said. "They'll stand better in the narrow confines of the catacombs anyway."

"How is she?" asked a gruff voice. A portly man with a vaguely trimmed beard walked up. He seemed only a little winded; maybe the portliness was all muscle.

"Her arm is broken," Thomas answered. "She said there will be more in the crypts. We need to take the fight to them, now."

"Devil of a thing, that fire," the other said. "Wouldn't mind having that down there with us..." He looked us both over, then took a step away. "We'll see what we can do, though."

I closed my eyes and laid back. I could hear the men gathering themselves and moving off across the garden. Thomas was away. My arm throbbed, my throat was still tender, and...I opened my eyes and raised my left hand: the fire was still there, damped now to a patient blue.

"Rae-Anna?" Thomas called hesitantly. I squinted at him. "Um...I'm wanting to splint your arm, but most of these sticks are too narrow or too twisted. Would you care if we used some of these...bones?"

My eyes went wide. He held two of them up—as examples, I guess—and shrugged helplessly. I was about to nod begrudgingly when, from the open door to the crypts, there came a single thump of a drumbeat.

We both looked. A second thump. A third, faster. It became a continuous beat. I heard Thomas cry out, and looked over as he dropped the bones. They bounced once, twice, rattled as they joined. Across the garden, all the shattered bones drew together. The army was rising again.

But the ash remained ash. I struggled to sit up, gasped as my right arm slipped down and the bones jostled. Thomas hurried to my side, sword ready. But he could not stand alone against all the undead the village men had slain. And if he did, all signs indicated the bones would simply reattach. As would the bones below where the men fought now.

Mahmoud emerged from the crypts at a run. I didn't blame him; this fight was not his. But instead of running for the gate he came to us. "Thomas, Rae-Anna," he said. "The fight goes badly." He looked me over, saw my arm still un-splinted. "She cannot help." His voice was flat. I could sense his despair, and a bit of his resignation.

But his presence gave me hope. The fire still burned patiently, waiting. I reached across, laying my hand gently where the bones were broken. "I wouldn't normally ask this," I whispered. "If the battle were over, I could rest. But it has only begun."

The fire spread like water, encircling my arm in a sort of tube. As it shimmered I expected to feel something; instead it returned to my hand, and the memory of the break was simply gone from my mind. I stood as Thomas and Mahmoud watched. The fire grew again, wakening.

"Just be sure my arm is never trapped," I said as I looked out over the re-resurrected army. It was not so many as I feared; a lot of bones went into making one skeleton. It was marvelous, really, the complexity of man.

Thomas and Mahmoud went ahead as the skeletons advanced, keeping them contained as I moved among them. No longer did their sword-strokes fell them. Bones chipped, shattered, were sent tumbling away. But whatever was left pressed on, until it came within my grasp.

I felt eyes, once, and looked up to see Mother Superior gazing out of one of the windows. Her hand clutched her crucifix, but whether she held it out toward me or toward the undead I couldn't tell. It didn't matter to me anymore.

The last of the skeletons burned to ash. The drumbeat continued, muffled below. We turned for the crypts. "What of the other Sisters?" Mahmoud asked.

"What of them?" I returned.

"Should we free them? They might be needed."

I glanced up again; the window was empty. "All they would do is pray to Our Father," I said. "And He is already here."

As we descended the stairs, we could hear the sounds of battle far ahead. "It will be harder, now, in tight quarters," I said. "But we need to do the same thing down here, if we can."

"Form a funnel," Mahmoud said. "The narrow end is you and

Thomas. The rest of us will push ahead, pressing the undead through the funnel until you can burn them."

Thomas and I exchanged glances. "That's...smart," Thomas said.

Mahmoud spared us a glance as we turned a corner. The sounds of battle were suddenly near. "I was not always a drover," he said simply.

My steps slowed as he went ahead, his scimitar held comfortably in his hands. He did not seem a mere drover, and I chided myself for ever thinking so.

We heard shouting; Mahmoud was relaying instructions. Thomas and I hurried ahead, and I joined the battle again.

It was disconcerting, at first. My breath came in short gasps, my mind reeling against the knowledge that the entire goal of all these brave, strong men with weapons was to funnel the enemy to me to handle. They would make it worse, actually, to strike the enemy down. Better the undead come to me whole, so every bone could be turned to ash.

After the first long minutes, though, I was too distracted to care. Too distracted to think. I think they began to sense what was wrong, to know I was the greater threat. Some of them came through the funnel unhampered, seeking me out. And they no longer simply blundered into my hands.

I could not believe how many there were. The corridor seemed full of bobbing skulls and grasping hands. The chant thrummed louder, the drums pulsing as if from the earthen walls themselves. The torches flickered. Bony fingers dragged at my sleeves, caught brief hold of my arm before popping in the heat and turning to ash. The floor was thick with the ash, and I stumbled again.

Several leapt on me—I couldn't count them for the number of bones clattering and pressing. Thomas shouted; I think men came to help. Somehow my fire-hand remained free and I waved it erratically, slapping as at spiders. The world became white bone and white fire. Ash burned my lungs.

Someone hauled me roughly to my feet; Thomas barked something at him, received a mumbled but defensive apology. I waved them both off as I blinked away dust and soot. The battle still pressed.

Just as the chant reached a crescendo, I felt a soothing radiating up from my hand through to my head, damping the sound. The echoes came to me as though through water. The men still battered at undead, my hand still reached out to burn, but I felt somehow distant. A mere observer.

The funnel poured out into a room. Four biers rose in the center, and the walls were lined with broken sarcophagi. Bruce stood with his three disciples, each beside a bier; the undead were gone.

Bruce glared at the men gathered against him. "Where are the Sisters?" he growled.

"Safe on the surface," I said.

He fixed me with his gaze. "My army will take care of them soon enough."

I shook my head. "I destroyed them all." His eyes widened, but only briefly. "Burned them to a crisp," I confirmed with a nod. "No resurrecting from that."

"'A little child shall lead them,' indeed," he said. "Such brave men, all, to lean on a willow wand."

"Supple. And unbreakable," I agreed calmly.

His eyes flashed, and he glanced around the room. I could tell he was trying to instill fear, but I saw a hunted look in those eyes. I began to pity him. "You still have your soul, don't you," I said. "Not quite in the flames of Abaddon, it persevered. And you've brought it back."

He leered. "I did. I imagine that shocked poor Mother Superior to see me alive and well."

"It might still be able to be saved."

His leer vanished. "And why would I want to do that?" he said flatly.

"You've glimpsed The Pit," I said. "If you go back, it will be worse. You've been given one last chance, Bruce. Well, perhaps you've stolen the chance, but it is still yours."

"And why," he sneered, "would I choose to go back to the arms of a god who so callously throws men into despair?"

"Did he throw you there?" I asked. "Or did you? You rejected Him, Bruce; not the other way around."

He looked slyly at me. "Oh, you've done a fair bit of rejecting too, haven't you? Still looking to get rid of that fire? Or do you think he'll forgive you for how ardently you fought against it?"

"If we are faithless, He remains faithful; He cannot deny Himself," I said, quoting the words the fire gave me. "I fought because of ignorance, and false counsel; you have chosen your path knowing full-well the goodness you rejected."

"You know this because you were there?" He snorted. "You judge me with as little knowledge as your forbears."

I cocked my head. "So you thought it was a righteous thing to sacrifice children?"

The hunted look returned to him. He licked his lips. "I was under compulsion!" he screamed. "I had no control over myself!"

"Are you under compulsion now?"

He bared his teeth in a rictus. "They made me do it!" he seethed, gesturing at the other monks. They glanced at him, startled but not denying his words. "It was not my fault, and I was shown no mercy.

No forgiveness. It wasn't my fault!"

His words rang and echoed, but bent themselves around me like water around a rock. He gasped, now, chest heaving as he glared at me. "Are you under compulsion now?" I repeated.

He snarled, and all four reached atop their biers and pulled free swords. There was a strange coordination in the way they moved. It seemed to me that only Bruce had free agency; the others were tied to him somehow.

They leapt forward, attacking whoever was nearest them. "Try to spare the others!" I shouted. "Only leave Bruce for me."

I needn't have worried: Bruce came directly toward me, sword flashing. I admit I had no plan, and whatever thoughts I had were sundered in the face of his assault. I flinched away, and his sword-tip nicked my cheek. Thomas stepped in and began a furious set of parries and strikes; I wondered where Thomas had learned them. Then I wondered where Bruce had learned them.

I moved around the edge, trying to get to the other side of Bruce to touch him. He circled, and Thomas moved to stand between us again. I couldn't fault him; I didn't mind steel between myself and Bruce's blade. But it also meant the fight might go on forever—or until Thomas died.

I heard a thud, and a grunt. I glanced quickly; one of the other monks had been subdued, alive. Another, though, lay headless on the ground. I saw the limbs begin to twitch, the arms levering the body toward a sitting position. I sprinted over; I had no doubt he would be reanimated. Headless, though, he could not be saved. I knelt, laid a hand on his arm. "I'm sorry," I whispered, as flames shot out of him and wreathed around his body. Just briefly it seemed as though the fire wrapped around a head. I could make out features: open eyes were closed in relief, and a deep sigh left the body as it sank to the floor. I prayed quietly; I didn't know if he could be saved, or under what compulsion he might have been. It was not for me to know the final thoughts of a man.

Thomas gave a choked cry through gritted teeth. I looked up, saw him clutching his sword arm, blood welling between his fingers. I stood quickly as Bruce came for me again. He drew back his arm, ready to put all his might into the blow.

For the weapons of our warfare are not carnal but mighty in God.

The blade flashed. I reached out my fire-hand. Sparks showered as the edge struck my palm; Bruce's arm quivered, his eyes went wide. I stepped forward, sliding my hand down the blade. "Are you under compulsion, now?" I asked the third time.

He gasped once. "No."

"Will you submit to Our Father's will?"

His teeth ground. He brought his other hand up to the hilt. His knuckles whitened and sinews stretched as he pulled on the blade. But the fire held it. "No!" he seethed.

I sighed and let my hand drop. Our eyes held each other, and I saw the fires of Abaddon flickering in his a moment before the Sacred Fire tore through him and he collapsed in a pile of ash.

I looked to Thomas, my vision blurring. He came to me, and wrapped me in his arms. The men around us were silent at first, then one coughed. We separated, and I looked over; they had detained the other two of Bruce's disciples. Bound, their heads hung low. The fire had ebbed, its fury seemed satiated.

"Are they alive?" I asked.

One of the villagers standing over one—Aderron I thought his name was—kicked his captive. As the man lurched and grunted, I held up a hand. "No," I said firmly. "I believe they were under compulsion, as Bruce had been. We must send them to trial first, and see what Our Father's will is regarding them."

The one who had been kicked looked up. I saw no hardness in his features, but I couldn't say if he was truly repentant. He didn't babble innocence, in fact he spoke not at all. He only looked at me a moment, glanced down at my acolyte's robes, then again at the floor.

"Well this is a fine mess," boomed a strong voice. I turned as Mother Superior swept in, the other Sisters close on her heels. She glanced around the room, her gaze resting on the two disciples for a moment, then at me. "I thought to find you here," she said curtly. "Rae-Anna, return to your cell until you are fetched."

Thomas stepped forward. "Now, wait!"

"How dare you?" Mother Superior hissed. "You forget your place!" Her gaze bore into him, and I could tell he quailed slightly; I did as well. She glared around the room, full of her power and authority. "We are of course grateful for the actions taken by you all, but this is still my convent and I intend to investigate matters as I choose. Do any of you question this?"

"Mother, I only meant to say—"

She cut him off with a dismissing chop of her hand. "You will have your time to speak, young man. If you want to be helpful, help these men take our captives to the surface."

An uncomfortable shuffling ran around the room, and no one moved to obey. "Beg forgiveness, Mother," said the mayor gruffly. "But young Thomas makes a fair if unspoken point; we all of us would be dead if not for Rae-Anna, and it don't seem right to treat her like a criminal."

I lowered my eyes. My heart leapt at their compliment and confidence, and that they would even stand up for me. But I had too many unanswered questions to share in it.

Let every soul be subject unto the higher powers.

I laid a hand on Thomas' arm and smiled at him briefly. I looked at Mother Superior and curtsied, then exited the chamber. My time would come. The time of the Fire would come.

Chapter 15

I sat in my cell as the sun lowered. I had left the door open; Mother Superior had not commanded it shut, and none of the Sisters who walked by contradicted it. So I watched as the men also helped clean up the gardens, shoveling ash into barrows and wheeling it through the gate. Occasionally a Sister would approach one, he would drop his shovel and follow her, and return some time later. Even Thomas was called away. He glanced through my open door, set his jaw, and followed. I imagined his spirited defense of my actions.

During that time, I also saw Mahmoud more than once. He seemed to still be Mother Superior's man, always running errands and messages. He, too, frequently glanced my way. And whenever he did, I found myself glancing away through the open gate. The convent then seemed to fade away, the cell falling behind as I made my way across far pastures and through darkening woods. All of my desires to find solace within the convent had vanished. Any longing for the Sisterhood was gone, replaced by an intense wanderlust—no, it was not quite that. I would not wander, but would go where I was directed. And something in Mahmoud's gaze or presence awakened it within me each time I considered him.

Thomas came back, his countenance dark. He worked his shovel with annoyance bordering on anger. His defense must not have gone well. I was not surprised. Nothing stood Mother Superior's back up more than a spirited defense.

And yet, what was I prepared to give? Would it matter? The worst—and best—she could do is throw me out. Perhaps in this new light, the worst she could do was order more penance. Order me locked up, or executed and buried without my left hand, or something. I feared more for her than for myself, if she tried to pronounce such a judgement. With the sentiment expressed by the men alone, the power of the convent would drastically wane if she did. Even without that, I did not think the fire would be well-pleased either.

And so I waited as the sky purpled. Finally Sister Lucy came, bearing a lamp. She only looked at me expectantly. I rose silently and followed.

We entered the Chapterhouse. A few of the Sisters turned to look; most kept their backs stiff. Mother Superior sat at the head, Sister Bethenny sat beside her, and after I was seated facing them across a space, Sister Lucy walked over and sat on her other side.

"We have convened to bring to trial the child Rae-Anna," Mother Superior intoned. A scurry ran through some of the Sisters; many had begun considering me a daughter. "We have heard much testimony already, with little conflict. However, it is inherently biased in one way or another—by gratitude or love." I flushed; I wasn't sure if Thomas' feelings should be called that just yet. "We will call upon Our Father and The Beloved to oversee these proceedings, that truth may hopefully come out. The censer."

I looked up as Sister Lucy picked the censer up from the table and uncapped it. She dusted in a pinch of incense, prayed, and held it out to Mother Superior. She too prayed a small incantation, then reached for the taper to light it.

As solemnly as the situation dictated, and without knowing why but believing, I raised my left hand and extended a fingertip. Mother Superior glanced at me, startled. The blue flame flickered on my finger a moment. Then, from across that space of some fifteen feet, a blue flame arose on the incense and the fragrant smoke curled heavenward.

Sister Lucy dropped the censer with a clatter as the room gasped. I felt I should be startled as well, and yet I calmly put my hand back under the table. The fire was gone—not just from my hand, but I knew that manifestation of what I was only now beginning to understand was also gone forever. The presence remained, but I would never see blue flame again.

"What will happen to the two men who were spared?" I asked in the silence.

"That is not your concern," Mother Superior said.

"They were under coercion; I gave Bruce a chance to repent, which he refused. They must have the same chance."

Mother Superior pressed her hands against the table, I was sure to still her trembling. She could not keep it far from her voice though. "I said, *child:* that is not your concern!"

"'Child'?" I echoed. "I faced an army of skeletons and undead, and through the power of the fire destroyed them all. Do you know I had to physically touch each one in order to do that? I had to be close enough to reach them with my hand—each one. Hundreds. No matter how they pressed around me, no matter how terrified I was or sickened by what Bruce had done to them, to Sister Aitrinn, to the men of the village. And still I am somehow a child?"

"We still do not know where this fire is from!" Mother Superior thundered. "For all we know this is only some first movement in a much larger attack against us, and against our Order."

I gaped at her. I couldn't help it. "Did not The Beloved teach: 'Every kingdom divided against itself is brought to desolation'? What could possibly be gained by raising this entire army and then destroying it after it has killed *one* Sister?"

"Trust. Trust in you, and whatever evil you bring into the world."

"Evil," I said flatly, disbelieving. "Evil? Evil that healed Mahmoud, that healed me, that strengthened and encouraged me and comforted me? That spoke the words of Our Father to me when my own thoughts went astray? That is what the Liar does?"

"We have only your word that it does those things," Sister Bethenny said. "At least, that it gave you comfort from the Sacred Words."

"I spoke them to you," I said. "I have not been among you long enough to memorize all those things, to deliver them at just the right time."

"We cannot allow you to roam free with this—whatever this thing is! Surely you see that?" Sister Lucy pleaded.

"The fire is gone," I said calmly. "It left after it lit the censer. And what I *see*, Sisters, is that you fear this thing because you cannot control it. Despite healings, despite comforts, despite saving you from the undead and from Bruce, you condemn it because it doesn't give you power. And it doesn't give you power because you reject it—because you cannot bend it to your will!" I couldn't help but laugh, though with a tinge of bitterness.

Mother Superior sniffed. "Well, we are not to seek power. That is not the purpose of wedding The Beloved."

"Indeed," I responded. "And yet here you sit, wreathed in power. What will you do with the two men that were not killed?"

"I said—" She cut off as I arched my brows, and gave a grumbling sigh. "They have done great evil. They must be punished."

"Will you at least give them the opportunity to renounce those ways?"

"And risk more lies? What if they confess what we wish to hear just because they fear death?"

"Even the thief hanging next to The Beloved confessed at the point of death, and he was promised to be in Paradise. It is not for us to choose salvation or damnation, but the Father alone."

Mother Superior glared at me warily. "By saying so you condemn the entire church," she said.

"Not the body of The Beloved," I replied. "Only those that would use their place in it to control those around them, because they have grown too comfortable. Not, as some of his followers, 'in journeyings often, in perils of waters, in perils of robbers, in perils by mine own countrymen, in perils by the heathen, in perils in the city, in perils in the wilderness, in perils in the sea, in perils among false brethren.'"

"And now you condemn us! We Sisters should all become itinerant, then? Offering no place of solace to the traveler in so many perils as you mention?"

"Of course not, Mother," I said humbly. "That is not what I meant to imply. I put in perhaps too much of my own feelings. And yet we have seen few travelers of late, haven't we? Few villagers even come to our doors, except to bring us offerings in return for some blessing or favor. Sister Lucy once told me that Bruce and the others stood as a warning against becoming that which we might abhor. They have warned us against great evil, to be sure; but what of insipid evil? What of the simple evil of a lethargy of calling? Of settling for the mere tasks that *must* be done, rather than striving for that which *could* be done through His power? Out of fear that maybe He won't actually do what He promised, out of the name of 'prudence,' we choose the safe road, the predictable road, instead of the road that surrenders all control." I paused, shaking my head. "For too long all I wanted was acceptance, a place to stay where people might love and care for me. Our Father has already provided that place, and it is in Him, and He is wherever He sends us. Oh, please, stay and be diligent if He has called you here. But don't damn as evil that which makes you merely uncomfortable or doesn't fit your mold. Or that which upsets you because it strikes your conscience."

Mother Superior sat silent a moment, gazing at the censer that still burned, though the fire now was a natural orange. "Many have lost their way, following the course you set," she said, almost absently.

"'But he that shall endure unto the end, the same shall be saved'," I replied.

She looked up. "And where has Our Father called you, then?"

I gave a slight shrug. "Out," I said. "Away from here—only because this is not where I belong. I do not know where yet."

Her eyes widened. "Alone? You're just a girl! A slip of a girl!"

I chuckled. "I doubt the villagers would agree—or the bones turned to ash, now dumped outside our walls."

Mother Superior took a deep breath. "It is hard to accept," she began.

"You don't have to," I said, harshly.

She fixed me with a stare. "It is hard to accept the rebuke you give," she said. I dropped my eyes. "I would feel better for you if you did not travel alone."

I looked up again, still smiling. "I'm not alone," I reminded her. Her jaw worked a little, and I held up a hand. "I understand your meaning, Mother, and I am grateful for your care. I do not believe I will travel by myself, though."

She glanced toward the door quickly, and when her gaze returned she goggled. "That, I think, would be most unseemly," she warned.

It would, I knew. But that was not a decision either of us were ready to make, yet. "Perhaps he will be my brother," I said. "In spirit," I amended quickly; no sense starting my mission with a lie.

"We will extend the offer of confession to Percival and Garrett," she said. "Yet we will guard them closely against treachery. Some prudence is permitted, I assume?"

"I would prefer it over bitterness," I replied.

She snorted. "Very well. In the matter of Rae-Anna's guilt over the events of the past several weeks; of her involvement in the coming of an old and terrible evil; of inciting desecration of Our Father's sacred home—how find we all?"

Swiftly, all left hands were raised: not guilty. I did not care which way it would have gone, but I appreciated that perhaps their opinions might change. But it struck me, too, that my innocence was admitted by the showing of the hand I had been cursed for.

I think Mother Superior appreciated it as well, as she took in the showing and her lips smirked. The hands were lowered. "Now, on supplying Rae-Anna with provisions and blessing into whatever environs Our Father sends her?" Unanimous right hands: support. "Then," she continued as she rose from her seat, "in the name of Our Father, The Beloved, and the Sacred Fire, we free Rae-Anna from commitment to our order, from any charge of guilt surrounding the last weeks, from any charge of curse for her handedness, and pray over her blessing and the Bread of the Road. We will, of course, provide her with some actual bread as well," she added with a smile. "We would not see a Sister in need and only wish her well, without supplying her physical needs. Such a faith would be worthless."

I bowed my head. "Thank you, Mother," I said—and I meant it.

It meant more than I thought it would, for her to add the part about my handedness. It's easy to say we find comfort in Our Father alone, and yet he gave us community for support. Now that I was prepared to leave it, it gave me great peace to know I left it not in anger or through rejection, but purely because I was called. Oh, I would have gone regardless. But His kingdom is one of unity, and discord saddens me—I believe righteously so. "I don't suppose," I said timidly, "that this Order might also have some outfits of the road?"

Mother Superior laughed, and the rest of the Sisters joined her. "I think we can find a few extra bolts of cloth. Let us make preparations as we need; you may depart and do the same."

I stood, made another curtsy, and left.

Outside, Thomas was in the midst of pacing away. When the door shut he spun quickly, lightning in his eyes as he darted forward, lamp in hand. It had become full-dark during my trial. "Well?" he asked.

"All is forgiven," I said, my chest fluttering. "The fire is gone, though, but the presence that manifested it is still here. It's the Spirit, Thomas, making known the mind of Our Father. He has blessed me with it—He wants to bless everyone with it, but they have to accept it and surrender to it. I think the Sisters are on their way, though they have a lot of tradition to clear out of the way of their minds."

He took a step back, blinking rapidly. "That's a lot," he said. "And nothing that I've heard before."

"I know," I said sadly. "But I think I am one of those He has asked to re-awaken many to that truth."

"So," he said, and his shoulders dropped a notch. "You'll stay here as a Sister and minister to whoever comes your way?"

I continued to smile at him as I shook my head. "This is too important for me to wait for people to come here," I said. "I'm going to have to go to them, seek them out."

Comprehension—and apprehension—came to his eyes. "Where?"

I giggled. "I don't know!" I said. In my mind I saw the broad fields outside the convent, the hills rolling away to an endless horizon. I saw mountains and rivers and seas—but I also saw dark clouds and storms, demons, ghosts, and evil spirits. I sobered. "I think this was only a prelude, Thomas. Great evil is breaking out everywhere. The fire will not come again, but I will be fighting many things worse than skeletons with whatever tools the Sacred Fire gives me. It will be dark and terrifying and incomprehensible at times. I do not know what roads across land or sea I will travel, will not know what shelter I will have." I shuddered as another vision flashed to mind. "I believe some shelter will actually be the very source of some of the evil I will fight, just as it was here. And instead of rest I will fall directly into the arms of whatever evil I have been sent to destroy." I felt a fire in my bones and I drew myself straighter. "And it will be the deadliest embrace—for the evil. In trying to destroy me, it will be destroyed," I said fiercely.

He nodded once, and his fingers flexed on the hilt at his side. "That's...a lot," he said again, though he grinned. "Do the Sisters send you out alone?"

"They only send me with blessing and provision; how I travel is up to me." In the silence, I felt a smile I couldn't keep in. "Knowing everything I just said, will you come with me?"

He took a deep breath. "I'm not sure how much use I'll be to you," he said. My mouth gaped, stunned. I hadn't expected that answer—and certainly not so swiftly. He continued before I could think of a response. "With everything you say you'll be facing—demons? Ghosts? What good will I be? I don't have this Sacred Fire you say you have. What good will *this* be?" He indicated his sword. "It seemed little use in the fight we had here."

I nodded once. "'*Not by might, nor by power, but by my spirit,*'" I agreed. "It spoke to you, on the bank of the river. The Sacred Fire sought you, too, and you sought it. Are you sure you don't have it?"

Thomas held up his hand, then yelped as it limned in blue fire only briefly. "Oh, that was weird," he quavered. "I didn't expect that to happen."

I couldn't help but laugh. "Don't feel too bad; I fainted the first time it happened to me."

"But how will it look, a young man and young woman traveling together—alone? And...unwed?"

I sighed. "Mother Superior wondered the same thing," I said. "I don't think...I mean, we could I suppose, but...I mean, do you think so?"

He considered a moment. "I care for you very much," he said earnestly. "I think—no, we *will*. I promise it. But..." He trailed off and his shoulders sagged. "There's still too much of what happened with Sister Judith..." He pressed his lips together, looking away.

"I don't hold that against you," I said quietly. "I know it was not your fault."

He fixed me with his gaze. "I know," he said. "And one day that will mean everything to me. It just doesn't help right now. Not yet."

I drew a sigh. I wondered if he struggled as much to forgive Sister Judith as I did. Probably far worse. We would both have to work through that on our own, else it would always stand between us. "I understand," I said. "My other suggestion was that we travel as brother and sister in The Beloved."

He glanced down at his hand, then at me. "That, I think we can do," he said. "It's not too close to deception, is it?"

I smiled. "Well, we'll have to work that out as we go, I guess."

"Great, then." He rubbed his hands together. "So when do we start this wonderful journey into the arms of great evil?"

I laughed, blessed already to have such a traveling-companion. "The Sisters have promised me provision, and a change of clothing. Probably tomorrow, though, if you'll be ready."

His smile faded. "I'll have to tell my father," he said.

Chapter 16

I awoke lazily the next morning, the sun already above the walls and shining throughout the garden. A blue jay screeched at some imagined offense. I blinked a few times before realizing I had not been woken for dawn prayers. I knew a knot of fear before remembering all that had changed, and realizing they would already consider me more of a guest than an acolyte—free to make my own schedule.

I sat up, worrying that thought. Free. Not even village or familial duties would hold me. And yet I was perhaps more bound than any slave, bound to obey The Beloved and whatever prompting of the Sacred Fire.

For this morning, though, there was little prompting except natural ones. I washed my face and completed ablutions. I sent up little prayers when my mind was not otherwise occupied. I strolled through the garden; little traces of ash remained here and there as reminders of the horror, but in a far-removed way. Soon enough, wind and rain and snow would wash even those last traces away.

I went to breakfast. Sister Bethenny smiled at me and gave me generous portions of oatmeal and bread, and even a small cup of milk. After I sat down, Sister Lucy came and sat across from me.

"You slept well?" she asked, not unkindly—as she might ask a guest.

I smiled. "I did, thank you. I didn't realize how tired I was."

"Do you know where you're going next?"

I considered as I swallowed a spoon of oatmeal. Sister Bethenny had even dashed in some cinnamon. I wondered if she was trying to get me to stay, and smiled. "Not specifically," I said. "I only sense that I will know when I know."

She laughed. "Well as long as you're sure," she said.

I laughed too, but also prayed. "Perhaps when Thomas returns, something will come to me then."

"When is he due back?"

I shrugged. "It depends on his father, I suppose, if there are any final tasks he would have him do, or how long he takes to pack."

"Speaking of, we have a few things ready for you. Sister Olivia should have put them in your room by now. Enough for a week, at least..." She trailed off, her mouth twisting apologetically. "We never were bountiful, here."

"I didn't think we were supposed to be," I said. "But it will be more than enough, and I'm grateful."

A tear glistened in her eye. "I did so much evil by you," she whispered.

I startled. "Sister, you were the kindest of all, to me."

She scoffed. "Yes, until it mattered the most. Easy to be kind to someone when there are no overt dangers of doing so."

"I cannot think Sister Judith made it easy for you."

"Yes, well, there's another point; perhaps I did it to spite her, more than to show you the love of The Beloved."

I smiled. "Perhaps, but Our Father used that to his advantage as well. All I know is your kindness and the love of The Beloved sustained me here, and gave me somewhere to go when I had doubts or questions. If there is judgement to be dealt for your motivations, it won't come from me."

She took a deep, quavering breath, smiled, and nodded. "You will write to us, let us know how Our Father is using you in the wide world?"

"Of course," I said. "As long as it won't tempt any of you away from your posts." We chuckled together. "Are all of you staying here, then?"

"We are. You spoke some hard words last night—true, but hard. It will take time for them to get into our hearts. For now we have sent the proclamation that the dormitories are re-opened for guests; our convent will once again be open to the weary traveler. And, fortunate for us, they are already cleaned and ready." She smiled hesitantly until I laughed, then joined me. I could hope for no better outcome from my labors.

Soon she left to attend some business, and I took some time to wander the cloister and halls, wandering through memories of only a few months, but what had seemed most of my life. Not because of drudgery or pain, though there had been some of that; but because through this place I was set on my course. Every small moment, nearly forgotten at the time, suddenly rang with importance now. And before I knew it, I found myself walking down the stairs into the catacombs.

A few men still worked down here. Most of the broken sarcophagi had been at least set in place, the shards carried away. Many a niche would be available for future dead, now. I had not time to notice before, but so many of the broken and empty alcoves had been martyrs and saints at which I had prayed fervently. Important, I had thought them. I suspected now they would not call themselves so. I wondered if Bruce had awoken them thinking they would be stronger in his army than regular people. He would have forgotten, as near as I could judge, that any great deeds they had done would have been born of their spirits, not their bones.

I arrived before long at the cave-in. Here the men were busiest, hauling dirt back to the surface in buckets lowered by ropes while others built a framework for a new roof. A few seemed tense as they worked, then relaxed when I approached. They cast wary eyes to the spots of blood still staining the floor where the strangers had sacrificed themselves to bring Bruce and his disciples back to life. I found myself studying those spots, wondering what if any compulsion had been laid on them as well. It didn't feel right, that anyone could be forced to commit evils they didn't want to.

Just then, one who seemed to be leading the work party approached me. "I thankee, Sister, for stopping by," he said, clutching his cap to his chest. "These men were powerful feared to be here alone."

"Oh, I'm..." I stopped myself from saying I wasn't a Sister. I had taken no vows, but what they sought in a Sister I was able to provide. "I'm glad to be of help. Tell me, did you know the men who died there?"

He quailed a moment, clutching his hat tighter as he made a warding motion. "I'm not part o' them the least, Sister."

I placed my hand on his shoulder and squeezed. "I didn't mean it that way, goodman. I only hoped to learn why they came here in the first place. No fault to you if you overheard something somewhere."

"Well no fault of a man if he finds hisself in the same room as others, is it? No fault if he hears something mebbe he doesn't like, something that sits off. No fault to him if he dassn't believe what he hears?"

I laughed easily. "My good man, if I had heard anything that sounded like what happened here, before it happened, I wouldn't have believed it either."

"It was like that, Sister, truly it was. At first it was just talk, you see. They'd come to see some of their old folk, knew they's buried nearby but din't know where, din't know how to find it. But they had strange faces, as my old nan would say; none of us wanted to talk to 'em. But...well, Sister, they bought us drinks. I'm sorrowed to say it. We sold your souls for a pint, Sister, and we're full-sorrowed by that. We didn't know, but we shoulda trusted. 'Cept it didn't seem really off at first. Just a friendly pint it was, at first."

"Again, my good man, no one could foresee what turned out. Did the men seem in their right minds, though? Did any of their actions seem...off? Other than having strange faces."

He shook his head solemnly. "No, Sister, they seemed like right men to me. Too eager, and sometimes too strange. Sometimes they slipped into a different language." He shuddered. "None I'd heard a'fore; but after, when we thought we'd lost, I heard it again. We all did. Them skeletons that came up with your departed Sister, they spoke it in that chant. Do you know what it was?"

I thought back, and nodded. "A language from the north," I said. "But it is not the language that makes men evil; that was only co-incidence. As to the words they chanted, I knew them: it was only various words that meant 'fire.'"

He fingered his cap. "'Fire,' miss?"

"Yes. I think they hoped to make me doubt the fire I carried, to believe it was something evil—or, that anyone else who understood their chant would think the fire I carried was evil. By speaking as though they were familiar with it, they could spread seeds of doubt."

The chamber went suddenly silent. I looked around as each man had stopped in his work and looked on me with a sort of intensity I couldn't understand. Those with caps now had them off, and clutched them.

"You don't...doubt the fire, do you?" the first man asked.

"After what it did?" I replied, a little alarmed.

He held up his hand. "Sorry, miss—Sister; we didn't mean it that way. We wouldn't want you thinking we doubted you, or the salvation you brought us, is all."

"Oh," I said, glancing around the circle again. A few men had stepped closer, and each studied me as though I were a loved sister whose chastity had been cast in doubt by a rogue. I imagined what kind of spirited defense they had all put up in my favor if asked by any of the Sisters, and I blushed. "Thank you, kind gentlemen; no, I don't believe it for a moment. And neither does Mother Superior. No, this salvation was brought by the Sacred Fire spoken of in the Words of Our Father—a quite literal manifestation of him."

The men chuckled, all smiles now. Most returned to their work. I spoke a few more parting words to the foreman, blessed them, and began making my way back to the surface.

I returned to my cell, and found the bundle left me by Sister Olivia. It would not be difficult to carry: one extra set of woolen stockings, an extra dress, a scarf, and a traveling cloak would all likely be worn together against the cold. In a small sack I had a few cheeses and fruits, dried; waybread; and a stick of sausage—I could only imagine Mother Superior had brought it back with her, we wouldn't have had something like that on hand. There was a collection of vegetables as well, mostly potatoes and a pepper or two. And, of course, a jar of oatmeal. A small feast if taken all at once. In the face of unknown days, weeks...I put the thought aside. As far as I knew, this journey was for my life. I could not possibly carry all of it on my back.

I started as the gate bell rang, and almost hurried to open the door before I remembered that would no longer be my duty. As I stood in the door to my cell, I saw Sister Jenneth hurry out and open the gates. There was a collection of men there, some I recognized from the village but also several others. I could not hear across the garden what was being said, but then I saw the laden donkeys outside. Travelers.

I strolled out, taking a seat on a bench to enjoy the warmth of the sun while I could. The donkeys were unloaded so they could be taken to the cow byre for stabling; the travelers were shown to the dormitories. One of the donkeys belonged to a villager, and carried supplies from the town to help feed the visitors—and the Sisters.

Bit by bit, each part of the group made their way through the gate and were sent where they were needed. For being out of practice, I thought the Sisters moved efficiently. Then finally, at the end of the procession with a pack on his back and a companionable smile, came Thomas.

I stood until I caught his eye, then smiled as I sat and waited for him to come. He sat down, thumped his bag to the ground, and grinned at me.

"So," he said, "what's the plan?"

"You already know it," I replied. "Go where He sends me."

"Do you know where that is, yet?"

My gaze drifted, listening for some prompting inside. There were almost endless places to go—though, the convent was near the sea so we would probably not go west? I dwelled a moment on the thought, but felt nothing. Perhaps the shadowed woods? If the harp had indeed become cursed as it passed through that place—and yet, I felt a healthy fear, that what evil might dwell there was beyond my faith to assail. I felt for the wind, as though we might be like a sailboat, but it was still. I began to grow a little nervous: it was not a promising start.

I felt Thomas shift, then look at me. "Why are you staring at him?" he asked—not jealously.

I blinked, realizing I was looking at Mahmoud as he stood with his donkeys near the gate, talking to Mother Superior. I rose and walked over; Thomas followed a little bit behind.

Mahmoud looked over as I approached. "Sister," he said, bowing slightly. "I think I did never thank you."

"Oh, I don't know if you needed to," I said. "Thank Our Father, it was his healing." I saw Mother Superior's lips tighten momentarily out of the corner of my eye. I wasn't sure I was completely comfortable with it either, honestly.

He nodded graciously, but said nothing. "You are traveling?" he asked, sparing a quick glance at Mother Superior.

"I...am," I said. "Are you returning to Algiers?"

"I make my way there," he said. "There are other destinations on the way."

"Would you care for two extra traveling companions?" I asked, holding a hand toward Thomas. "We'll provide our own way."

He glanced at Thomas, down at his sword, then at me. His dark eyes searched mine for a time. "You are sure?"

I felt a tug this time, and nodded certainly. "It may not be all the way to Algiers, but we would go with you for a time at least."

He considered me a moment longer, and I could see some sort of apprehension in his eyes as he glanced again at Mother Superior. "You know I and my fathers and fathers' fathers serve Allah," he said quietly.

I smiled gently. "Mahmoud, I will not be able to help but speak of the love of Our Father or The Beloved, or withhold the working of the Sacred Fire as he works through me—for that is the very purpose of my journey. But it is not my intention to beat you into submission to His will. If you convert it will be because you cannot deny His workings, not because you have tired of hearing me and wish me to shut up."

I saw the apprehension leave his eyes and a measure of respect replace it. "With this agreement then, are you ready to leave?"

"I only need to get my pack from my cell," I said. When he nodded I went back and took it up from the cot. I paused a moment, looking at The Beloved on the wall, and glancing around the room I had become so familiar with in so short a time. For a moment I felt nearly weightless, about to be cast adrift on the winds with no inkling of where or even if I would land. There would be no single place I could go back to each night, no familiar room or even bed. Nowhere to settle, nowhere to get comfortable with, nowhere to learn all the nooks and alcoves and secret places. And, for a moment, I quailed.

But I realized it was not true. I would be in The Beloved's arms. No matter where I was I could return to his embrace each night. I could settle in his presence, become comfortable with his voice, could learn aspects of him I had never known. I would not be adrift, but would rather be anchored firmly to him everywhere at all times. I settled the pack on my back, closed the door to the cell, and returned across the garden.

Thomas and Mahmoud had moved outside the gate and stood waiting for me on the narrow track that led to the village. I paused beside Mother Superior. "Thank you, for everything," I said. "For taking me in when I was afraid, and giving me a place to learn about

The Beloved."

She gazed at me a long moment. "You will always have a place here, if you choose to return."

I could see the doubt written on her features. Mine was not a life she had considered, I could see. I didn't blame her, but it still hurt a little. She assumed I would be back, perhaps very shortly. I held back a sigh. "Thank you," I said instead, and managed a smile. I felt the tug again. If I returned, it would be my own failure to follow through, not because I had not heard my calling right. I sent a quick prayer against my weakness, and left the convent.

Thomas and I walked at the back of the mule train silently for a time. We would pick up the road south from Holden and make our way deeper into the countryside stopping at whatever hamlet, village, or city presented itself. I would be lying to say it still did not frighten me every now and again to think of it.

But then I would look at Thomas. He walked confidently, eyes almost always forward unless he was glancing at me. I did not know if doubt swirled through his mind as much as mine, but if it did he did not show it. Between his posture and the comfort of the Sacred Fire, my feet carried me forward.

It was warm for autumn, with a bright sun in a clear blue sky, blessing our journey. And yet, on the horizon, storm clouds were gathering, casting a shadow on the land ahead.

Scripture References

Chapter 4:

"Ye shall not live by bread alone." Deut. 8:3, Matt. 4:4

"I will not leave you comfortless." John 14:18

"Ye know me; for I dwelleth with you and shall be in you." John 14:20

"The world cannot receive me, because it seeth me not, neither knoweth me." John 14:17

"Because he lives, ye shall live also." John 14:19

"I defend the poor and fatherless, and do justice to the afflicted and needy." Psa. 82:3

Chapter 5:

"The world cannot receive me, because it seeth me not, neither knoweth me." John 14:17

"Not every one that saith, Lord, Lord, shall enter into the kingdom; but he that doeth the will of Our Father." Matt. 7:21

"Ye shall not afflict any widow, or fatherless child. If thou afflict them in any wise, and they cry at all unto me, I will surely hear their cry; and my wrath shall wax hot." Ex. 22:22

"'Father, forgive them: for they know not what they do.'" Luke 23:34

"'What I do thou knowest not now; but thou shalt know hereaft er.'" John 13:7

Chapter 6:

"Forbid him not, to come unto me." Matt. 19:14

"I am come to send fire on the earth; and what will I, if it be already kindled?" Luke 12:49

"He that hath my commandments, and keepeth them, he it is that loveth me: and he that loveth me shall be loved of my Father, and I will love him, and will manifest myself to him." John 14:21

Chapter 7:

Parable of Tares and Wheat. Matt. 13:24-30

Chapter 9:

"For our God is a consuming fire." Heb. 12:29

Chapter 11:

"Take no thought how or what ye shall speak; for it shall be given you in that same hour." Matt. 10:19

Chapter 12:

"With his stripes, we are healed." Isa. 53:5

Chapter 14:

"If we are faithless, He remains faithful; He cannot deny Himself." 2 Tim. 2:13

"For the weapons of our warfare are not carnal but mighty in God." 2 Cor. 10:4

"Let every soul be subject unto the higher powers." Rom. 13:1

Chapter 15:

"'Every kingdom divided against itself is brought to desolation.'" Matt. 12:25

"...in journeyings often, in perils of waters, in perils of robbers, in perils by mine own countrymen, in perils by the heathen, in perils in the city, in perils in the wilderness, in perils in the sea, in perils among false brethren." 2 Cor. 11:26

"'But he that shall endure unto the end, the same shall be saved.'" Matt 24:13

"We would not see a Sister in need and only wish her well, without supplying her physical needs. Such a faith would be worthless." *see* 1 John 3:17; James 2:15-17, 20

"Not by might, nor by power, but by my spirit..." Zech. 4:6

Prayer Times

Pre-Dawn—Nebuls

Dawn—Gemmans

Morning—Quard

Noon meal—Lentus

Afternoon—Aratus

Dinner—Scuros

Nightfall—Lunens

Midnight—Somnus

Acknowledgements

Time again to remember all who made this thing possible:

My Alphas and Betas, for their eager anticipation of drafts, and critical early opinions.

The Faith Family Writer's Group, and their gentle, sensitive opinions as they ruthlessly erase all my semicolons.

The coordinators and designers at GetCovers for a thrilling cover.

My ARC readers and reviewers who generously gave of their time to help the launch of this book.

And, of course, my wife and family for continued support and devotion, and letting me leave the house for a few hours to get this done.

About the Author

Daniel Dydek is a multi-genre author with his sweeping epic fantasy series The Triumvirs, and his supernatural suspense series, Spirit Wind, has already garnered two Finalist awards from Realm Makers. Besides writing, he also enjoys a personal relationship with Jesus Christ, mountain biking, reading, coffee shops, book stores, and Durango Colorado. He lives in Canton Ohio with his wife and son and two cats.

Support for the Author

First, thank you for reading this story on whichever medium you chose—Kindle, KU, or paperback. Your support means dreams come true! If you loved the story, there are a lot of ways to continue supporting the author FOR FREE. Here's a few:

1. Subscribe to the newsletter on danieldydek.com

2. Tell your friends!

3. Leave a review on Goodreads, Amazon, Barnes & Noble, or on your social media. (This is probably the greatest support of all, because we love hearing what people enjoyed about the book! Plus, you know, algorithms...)

4. Request your local library to get a copy

All these things help promote the books, and encourage the author to keep writing stories you'll love!

—The Beorn Publishing Team

The Triumvirs epic fantasy series

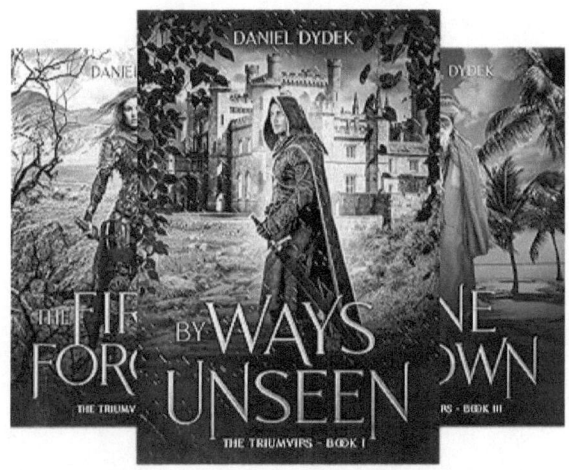

Centuries ago, the world of Oren was ravaged by uncontrolled magic during the Wizards War. In the wake of such devastation and evil, the God of All took three wizards and established for them a Room, of darkness and consciousness, and placed before them a great table whose appearance is of translucent slate, through which they might call up visions of the lands, entering when needed. Few even know these former wizards exist, and their work will always be credited to brave men and women of the world who were faithful in their obedience.

These wizards' task is keeping the peace, of prompting action against the forces of evil. They answer still to the God of All, but retain autonomy. He named them The Triumvirate, and over the centuries twenty-two Triumvirs have guided Oren through wars, famines, pestilences, and the rising and falling of countless empires.

Now, in this current Age of men, will come their most difficult battle.

Amazon search: The Triumvirs Dydek

Spirit Wind Christian suspense series

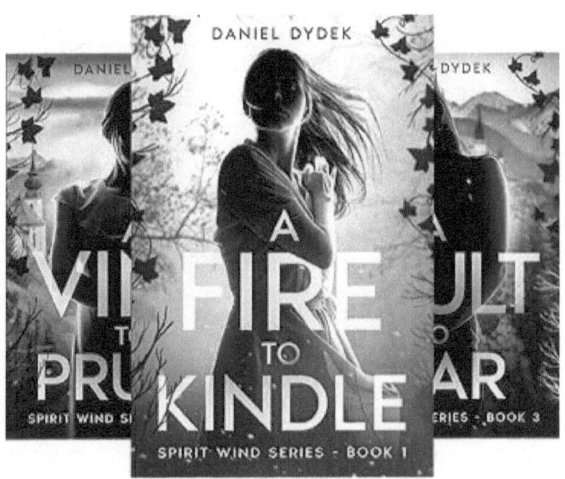

Cursed with left-handedness, then cursed with fire.

Except the fire seems to comfort, to strengthen, to speak wisdom. Wisdom like:

"The wind bloweth where it listeth, and thou hearest the sound thereof, but canst not tell whence it cometh, and whither it goeth: so is every one that is born of the Spirit."

And so Rae-Anna is borne on itinerant winds, never knowing what danger she'll be asked to face. But she knows this: it will always be demonic. And she will never be alone.

Amazon search: Spirit Wind Dydek

www.ingramcontent.com/pod-product-compliance
Lightning Source LLC
Chambersburg PA
CBHW031309280626
47169CB00017B/1163